SOON TO BE A MAJOR MOTION PICTURE

In Jonathan Keates' dazzling and superbly entertaining collection of stories, familiar scenes are shot from odd angles. A mighty angel arrives in a young girl's bedroom, watched by a terrified cat; a bored young wife in Aix-les-Bains takes a lover who fancies her clothes; an Italian boy in knickerbockers steals cherries and plunges into hot adult secrets. These tales, and many others, transport us to different periods, places and personalities – from a predatory American dowager in Venice to a correct gay couple in Clapham. And everyone secretly longs to be someone else.

The delicate, sophisticated surface of Keates's fiction is allied to a shrewd and humane attention to intricate emotions: desire and envy, concealment and revelation. These are stories that delight and disturb, combining a disconcerting power with the seductive charm of the cinema screen.

JONATHAN KEATES teaches at the City of London School. His earlier volume of short stories, *Allegro Postillions*, won both the James Tait Black Memorial Prize and the Hawthornden Prize. He has also written a novel, *The Strangers' Gallery*, a travel book, *Italian Journeys*, and acclaimed biographies of Handel, Stendhal and Purcell.

Soon to Be a Major Motion Picture

Fiction

Allegro Postillions

The Stranger's Gallery

Non-fiction

Handel: The Man and His Music

Stendhal: A Biography

Purcell: A Biography

Tuscany

Umbria

Italian Journeys

Soon to Be a Major Motion Picture

Jonathan Keates

Chatto & Windus
LONDON

First published in 1997

1 3 5 7 9 10 8 6 4 2

Copyright © 1997 by Jonathan Keates
'The Gift of Flight' first appeared in *Cold Comfort*, ed. James Loader,
© Serpent's Tail Ltd, 1995

Jonathan Keates has asserted his right under the Copyright, Designs and
Patents Act, 1988 to be identified as the author of this work

First published in Great Britain in 1997 by
Chatto & Windus Limited
Random House, 20 Vauxhall Bridge Road,
London SW1V 2SA

Random House Australia (Pty) Limited
20 Alfred Street, Milsons Point, Sydney
New South Wales 2061, Australia

Random House New Zealand Limited
18 Poland Road, Glenfield
Auckland 10, New Zealand

Random House South Africa (Pty) Limited
P O Box 337, Bergvlei, South Africa

Random House UK Limited Reg. No. 954009

Papers used by Random House UK Limited are natural, recyclable
products made form wood grown in sustainable forests. The
manufacturing processes conform to the environmental regulations of the
country of origin

A CIP catalogue record for this book
is available from the British Library

ISBN: 0 7011 6618 5

Contents

The Gift of Flight

The cat, in terror, bounces through the room. She too, he is disappointed to perceive, is more than a little afraid. He has wanted her to know that he would come, has hoped that in some way or other a dream, a premonition, a nudge or two of fantasy, might cause her to long for his arrival. Not, you understand, because he is especially vain of the effects he can produce. These are always taken for granted. It is simply that he wants her to have something in the way of an imagination, and at this moment, his wings still beating in great slow sweeps as he circles for a perfect landing, he is dreadfully afraid that she possesses nothing of the kind.

The landing has to be perfect, though he fancies it would make little impression on her if he crashed clumsily to the ground and slithered a short way across the floor. Hovering yet he takes mournful stock of the room, noting the hospital corners with which the bedcovers are tucked in, the careful arrangement of her slippers, the clean towel on the peg, and the small array of books on the shelf. He is quite sure, without looking at them, that they are not the sort of books which he would want to read.

She herself was reading when he flew in through the window. This was the act in which it was necessary for her to be caught. Of course he would have preferred to find her doing something more clandestine, sniffing an armpit perhaps, sliding an absent-minded finger up one nostril, scratching a spot and maybe cracking the scab between her teeth, but such things lack the kid of grace she is intended at this moment to express.

Circling for a last time, he notices the bowl of flowers standing precisely within the space where he had meant to touch ground. If he believed her capable of such deviousness, he would have supposed she had put it there on purpose. He doesn't know which irks him more, the vase itself, full of lilies, a plant he has always disliked for its brutal obviousness, or the disappointing realisation that its presence in this spot on the floor is not deliberate.

Of course, he knows why they have to be there, just as he knows why she pores over her book, and why, at this moment while his huge wings, which the room seems almost not to hold, make a final and, he has to admit, quite superfluous clap, she is turning away her head in a little wincing motion, her hands upraised, their palms turned outward, pressing against the air upon which, lightly, always lightly, he sinks to earth.

As if, in any case, he would touch her! It must spoil the impact his accomplishments have taught him to aim for. So he wants the hands upraised, yes, but in a different position, one which will say 'Goodness, that's wonderful!' or 'How cleverly you do it!' as his beautiful feet slide silently along the floor and his feathers rustle slightly before the wings settle into stillness. In short, he'd like her to envy him. Not everyone, he knows, can fly.

He has heard envy described as a tenth-rate emotion, something to be ashamed of, but he does not believe this. For him it offers another kind of fancy, an act of desire which, at its most intense, re-creates those who feel it in the very essence of what they best long for. He has heard a story – and he'd tell it her, if only she would ask – of the man who, when he understood what he supposed to be love was actually envy, murdered his lover, flayed the skin from the body and wrapped himself within it.

She won't ask this, insistently, maddeningly won't want to

know how he does what he does, how he launches himself into the air, how he flutters and swoops, his intrusive soaring integral to moments of salvation and epiphany. For an instant he wonders whether it was his beauty that frightened her, the whiteness of his skin, his thin fingers, the gleam of the reddish curls bouncing across his shoulders as he collects himself into the appropriate posture of reverence. He takes this inextinguishable radiance so much for granted that the effect it produces is now and then embarrassing. Things have happened in the past, in situations like this, which made him leave him a hurry.

But evidently it is not such effulgence which makes an impression. So why does she continue to turn away from him, in what looks suspiciously like humility? If there is one thing he can't stand, it is humility. He himself is a complete stranger to it, if only because it was left out – on purpose, he must assume – of the selective emotional kit with which he was originally furnished. A reliable measure of indifference to his own sublimity makes her abject cowering alien to him, almost nauseating.

Thinking about it later, when airborne and remote, he will blame this disgust for the subsequent banality to which he now falls in telling her not to be afraid. For fear, he starts to perceive, is what defines her. It is perhaps the closest she will ever come to the act of imagination so hugely absent in the *mise-en-scène*. She and the wretched skittering cat at the beginning are one creature – only the cat, he suspects, has more independence. Throwing back his beautiful curls with the merest little toss of impatience and contempt, and giving a light twitch to the tips of his wings, he lets his solemn glance travel round the room once again, reading a fear into each proof of neatness, the dreadful symmetry of those slippers, the way whereby the towel has been made to hang so that its corners match one another, the disposition of the books according to height, and the smooth, hard-edged bedclothes which, if he rapped his knuckles against them, might produce the dull ring of sheet metal. Order is a kind of fear, and he has always been above that sort of thing.

Almost wearily then, he begins his message to her, the form of words carefully rehearsed regardless of whether or not she is likely to pay any attention to its incidental stylish graces. Or rather, he hears himself deliver it, hears the words in disparate groups, over whose tone and colour he lingers with something suspiciously like impertinence, as though testing her reactions. 'Found favour', 'conceive', 'his name', 'unto him the throne', 'and of his kingdom'. She does not raise her head.

She does not raise her head, but she does venture a question, at the mere fact of which he is pardonably surprised. The good impression lasts only a moment, however, before an inherent sense of the commonplace sweeps everything else away, and he answers her as if he were talking to a child. The greatest intrinsic irony in the role he performs is that he himself should find innocence so unappealing. You'd have thought to detect, in the light he casts about him, in the sheen of his feathers and the deep luminosity of his large eyes (whose colour she will not remember, only think of as 'burning' or some such imprecise word), the image of a perfect candour, without shadow or ambiguity. Yet it is exactly this he has wanted all along to avoid. He piques himself on being able to inject, even into the simplest address, some humour of the quizzical, a note or two which will strike the hearer in such a way that, after the air has settled again from the last clap of his wings, there will be things left riddling and unclear.

With her this is impossible. Possibility, indeed, lay at the root of that obtuse question she asked earlier, one he was obliged to answer with such condescending directness. Her failure – or the sense he has of it – to grasp anything but the absoluteness of a a final reality suddenly makes him feel that she has no perspective, that the room behind her, the arched alcove with the bed in it, the bookshelf across one of whose sides the sunlight slopes, are all in some way flat, without dimension or tangible physicality. Perhaps it is merely that her dreadful acquiescence, insisting on nothing beyond what words and things vouchsafe in the form of immediately comprehensible meaning, has created a new system of space and proportion, one in which his gift of flight can no longer hold its place.

We believe, though we cannot be sure, that this was why he lied to her. It counts as lying, though some may view it as a sympathetic omission. For there is another part to his message – more strictly speaking, it is two parts connected to each other – which at this point somehow gets lost, like those additional layers of significance which are always said to disappear in the course of a translation.

He was going to talk to her, you see, about death, was going to share with her everything he had imagined regarding it, this particular special dying, an agony he has experienced vicariously, not through the medium of compassion, but by virtue – if only she were able to understand this – of the extraordinary skill he has in flying. In the beating of his wings he has seen that death, the skin steamed with sweat, the blood-matted hair, the ruthless incompetence with which the feet have been spiked together, and the attempt someone makes at delivering a *coup de gra–ce* (in charity or in anger? he isn't yet clear on this point) through a deep wound to one side of the torso.

He has tried to feel these things for himself as he flies, the passion and energy which went into their deliberate creation, as if the body had been a subject for discriminations in colour, texture and arrangement, a matter for art which he, beyond everyone else, would understand. In a manner he has watched over the completeness of her misery, her bewilderment of loss, the terrible resignation with which she has stood, another beside her, while the dying man hangs there talking to her, the almost automatic fashion in which she and her companions prepare the body for burial and the way whereby, after this moment, she appears to be forgotten, none of the texts making any significant mention of her in their anxiety to communicate the very curious nature of what happened next.

His profound sense of decorum has entered so far into the spirit of the whole occasion, with its storm and darkness contributing touches of the pathetic fallacy, that he feels as if entitled to a share in her emotions. He will not go so far as to shed tears – nature denies him that specific reaction – but he might claim, hand on heart, that he knows how she feels. On her behalf his mouth has opened in those soundless cries that rage against absence. Mimicking what he fancies she ought to say, he has had various of those dismal phantom conversations which assume the presence of somebody else to whom along the chosen words could have been addressed. In flying, he has noticed, for her sake, details scattered here and there, like the tones and branches gathered into a mysterious referential order by savage magicians, half their meaning lost now because one of the two people who could interpret them properly has died. And when the other dies, we shall be left either with the mere sticks and stones or else with the apparatus of a garbled rhetoric from which issues a holiness imperfectly understood.

She looks at him now, her eyes full of that same acquiescence which sickened him earlier. At this moment, however, a different feeling altogether steals upon him, a sudden wave of longing, accountable only in terms of something he is eager to add to his collection, not necessarily for the thing itself but for the satisfaction of possessing it. He longs, in this instant, absolutely to be her. He wants to know, with his particular species of devouring curiosity, how it is possible to exist within the limits set by a complete ignorance of what follows. The burden of vicarious pain he has carried, the whole laborious episodic death, the smell of it, the untidiness, the sense, as with every death, of a lingering irritation on the part of the dead themselves because there was something they still had left to do and were peremptorily interrupted in the process of doing it, these things are so conspicuously not there in the glance she raised, however furtively, to meet his unpitying eyes. And it is that very ignorance he feels he must master, as part of his rhetoric of borrowed and imagined emotion, because he never knew its power until now.

Consumed with this new desire, he scarcely listens to her final submissive acceptance of his message – of that fragment, at least, which he has designed to convey. His wings flutter with a renewed pevishness to depart, and taking care not to upset the lily vase, he mounts to the window, too preoccupied even to carry out the little circuit of the room which good manners, under ordinary circumstances, require him to perform as an earnest of his special nature. How can she? How can she fail to see, fastened within this promise he has given, never again to be made or hoped for, the truth of an ineluctable mortality? Perhaps it is because, as he tells himself with epigrammatic smugness, all imagination prefigures death.

Brooding still, he mingles with the blaze of morning. Only when aloft and serenely airborne does he recall the other part of his message purposely kept from her, the part which he had originally so looked forward to delivering as an ironic denouement, an and-now-for-my-last-trick turning tragedy into tragicomedy. He might have done it as he made ready to fly out of the room, in the purest expression of *esprit d'escalier*, if he hadn't been so captivated by that radiant obtuseness of hers. For it was rather a case of 'tarry a little, there is something else'. He was going to tell her, had he only remembered, about what happened at the very end, about the way in which the body disappeared, then came back alive – the oddest thing! – and spoke to people and let them touch it, in an ultimate trouncing of death. Something in the nature of a gift. A bit like flying.

Imagine Her Surprise

At the start of their second week in Aix-les-Bains Dolly's life became eventful in ways which even her natural common sense could scarcely account for. She quarrelled with Calixte – something that had happened only once or twice before in five years of marriage – over the loss of a brooch at the Villa des Fleurs about which he had insisted on informing the police. Spraining her ankle while getting out of a taxi, she spent an entire day fuming on the sofa while Calixte much too emphatically refused to go to the concert without her. Feeling better the next day, she went to the Casino and lost 150 francs and had her gloves stolen in the ladies' cloakroom.

She returned to be told something that made her even more angry with Calixte.

'Where's Victorine?' she asked. 'I told her to collect my hat from Laprade.'

'Oh, I said she might as well go straight away if she was going at all. A question of trains.'

'Go where?'

'Her mother's ill. Dying, probably. Don't look so surprised, it happens from time to time.'

'I suppose you imagine I'm the sort of woman who doesn't think her maid has a mother,' said Dolly crossly. Something of this kind had indeed suggested itself to her, but her better judgement had quickly suggested itself to her, but her better judgement had quickly suppressed the thought, and she was irritated that her husband seemed to know her so well. 'Why

8

did you let her go? Why couldn't you have waited until I got home and she could tell me herself? She's my maid, not yours.'

Calixte smiled. 'I like the idea of me with a maid. Anyway, she didn't seem to know how long it would be, but she said she'd get back as soon as she could. Nantes is an awfully long way off, but she seemed to think you'd manage.' Dolly was silent. 'Well, you did before, when she had scarlet fever.'

'That was different. She might never come back, one doesn't know how it is with those girls. Oh, I wish you hadn't not without asking me first!'

She felt the defences of rational objection beginning to crumble. It wasn't poor Victorine and her dying mother who really annoyed her, but Calixte's mocking serenity as he sat with his head on one side surveying her confusion.

'Your dresses arrived from Paquin. And those shoes you ordered before we left.'

He wanted to cheer her up. She looked at the boxes lying chastely unwrapped on the sofa, but did not race to open them. Calixte came and put both his arms lightly around her. 'My poor love, are you unhappy?'

After a while he began making love to her with an intense, single-minded professionalism, like a piano-tuner or one of those people who come in to wax the floors before a party. Ordinarily Dolly enjoyed it thus: her husband was serious in the same radiantly direct fashion that he was good-looking, and this species of physical authenticity flattered her judgement. This afternoon, however, there was something ambiguous in the way he touched her, as if wanting to tell her things she was too stupid to guess but ought nevertheless to know. Other women had told her how men used love-making as a form of blackmail, but it was only on occasions like this that she ever felt disposed to believe it.

For a while they lay without speaking. Dolly listened to the whirring sound made by a lawnmower outside the window, finding it curiously reassuring. Finally Calixte sat up and propped his elbow comfortably on the pillow, a position which suggested he had something to announce.

'You're leaving me, aren't you?' she said resignedly.

'For a week, yes.'

'Well, I didn't imagine it would be for good. Or that you and Victorine were having an affair.' Lying there, she kept him fixed within her gaze. 'You could have told me earlier, I wouldn't have minded.'

He turned his head away in embarrassment. She wondered if he was actually hurt.

'Why?'

'Something to do with the manager in Lille. Hervé telephoned me this morning while you were out shopping.'

'Lille will be perfectly ghastly in this heat. Or perhaps it'll be raining, in which case it'll be merely ghastly as usual. Don't go, stay with me.'

'I'll be back in a few days, I promise.'

No you won't, she thought, nobody's ever been back in a few days when they know someone is waiting for them.

'What am I going to do?'

'I've told Freddy and Elvire to look after you. I said that if they didn't we wouldn't take them to Etretat next year. Freddy gave me his word of honour.'

Dolly snorted. 'Freddy's word of honour is like one of those things Greek philosophers looked for and never discovered, and because they never discovered them everybody said how extra specially clever they were.'

Laughing, Calixte lowered his head to let Dolly stroke his hair. 'Forgive me,' he said, 'I'll feel even more guilty if you don't enjoy yourself.'

'I wish I were cynical.'

'Good heavens, why?'

'So that I could do something about your devastating sincerity. It makes women more secure to feel that men don't mean what they say.' She gave his hair a valedictory ruffle, kissed his forehead as though he were a child she were saying goodnight to, then sprang out of bed, threw off her peignoir and began opening the dress boxes on the sofa.

'I suppose these will have to keep me happy. Though their charms will rather have worn off by the time you get back.'

'Now you're as cynical as the rest,' laughed Calixte.

But Dolly wasn't listening. She was shaking out first one dress, then the next, then another, in horrified astonishment. They weren't hers at all. The colours were wrong, they were for somebody taller than she would ever be, the busts were too small yet the shoulders were enormous, a bricklayer's or a coal-heaver's. Yet there was no name save her own on the boxes.

With the shoes it was the same. She made a noise of disgust as she pressed them back into their paper nests, as if some baleful magic would cause them to hatch out as monsters to attack her. In their very presence there was something sinister, let alone in the fact that they came from Gavotte, where she always bought her shoes and the shop kept her measurement. She wanted to cry at the mockery of it all.

'What size are they?'

'I don't know, twice as big as mine, and hideous too. Oh, it's the beastly limit!'

'Perhaps I ordered them for myself. And the dresses.'

'Don't laugh, it isn't funny.'

'I might well have done, I'm getting fearfully absent-minded these days.'

Helplessly Dolly contemplated the parcels, so deceitful and menacing. Then she looked at Calixte, sprawled on the edge of the bed, one side of his body still covered by the sheet, giving him the air of being the very youngest of those Greek philosophers she'd spoken of earlier.

He threw it aside and crossed the room towards her. Pressing her face against him, shutting out the boxes and the sofa, he murmured: 'I'll make it up to you.'

She knew he would. The smell of cut grass drifted through the window as the lawnmower clicked and whirred outside.

'You're surely not going to send them back?' said Elvire. 'At least the dresses could be altered.'

'I'd have sent them today only I forgot, with Calixte leaving. You've no idea how frightful they are, I can't believe anything so grotesque ever walked out of Paquin. One is a kind of dark beige criss-cross affair, which looks like a lot of old weeds, and the other – goodness, you should see it! – is a cream-coloured baptiste smock, the sort of thing you might give to a niece with religious mania. She'd have to be large, mind you, and have feet the size of canoes.'

'I don't suppose . . .'

'No, absolutely not. I know you insist you're bigger than I am, but the effect would be absurd. Besides, our friendship would have to end. I couldn't possibly be seen with somebody dressed like a giant beatified niece.'

The two women laughed a little more uproariously because they were alone together. Freddy having been left behind at the Regina to play bridge with some English people he had taken a shine to, Elvire had swept up Dolly in the wake of Calixte's departure and carried her off to the Grand Cercle for the evening.

Barely tolerable throughout the afternoon, during which Dolly had dozed sulkily, the heat gave a palpable quality to the night air which made her restless and excited.

'Do you think I ought to have enjoyed that so much?' she said to Elvire as they finished dinner to the strains of the 'Nailavalse' and the ministrations of an over-solicitous waiter, whom they finally succeeded in staring out of countenance.

Elvire had a way of smiling which was both winsome and faintly corrupting, like a signal towards the fulfilment of her friends' most self-indulgent wishes.

'Do you want me to tell you that you ought to have spent the evening in an armchair at the Splendide with your petit point, like Penelope waiting for Ulysses to come back from Troy?'

'Ulysses was away for ten years.'

'Precisely, and Calixte will be gone for a week at the most, so you've no right to feel miserable. As for enjoying a good dinner, why on earth not? There's no law that says you have to pine like a little dog because your husband's away. Now, how are you going to amuse yourself, do tell?'

Dolly was silent. It embarrassed her to have to admit to anyone as perpetually calculating as Elvire that she had hardly given the matter any thought beyond the vague prospect of a circumscribed dullness ordained by Calixte's absence, Elvire, guessing as much, surveyed her critically.

'I may as well tell you at once', she announced, 'that Freddy and I haven't the slightest intention of looking after you. We're driving to Annecy tomorrow and won't be back until Tuesday. If you want to come with us you can, but . . .'

'No, thanks,' said Dolly curtly, disinclined to show her real annoyance, 'I'll stay at the hotel and read.'

'Nonsense! And don't get crabby with me when I'm treating you to such a nice dinner. I know we made Calixte a sacred promise, but you're a married woman and old enough to look after yourself. Have an affair or something.'

'What!'

'Oh, I don't mean that kind of thing, but a fling or two never did any harm, you know that. Only you've jolly well got to tell me all about it.'

The notion was so remote from Dolly's ideas of how her forthcoming days were to be spent that she burst out laughing.

'Where to begin?'

'Everybody knows where to begin if they really want some fun. Half the women in this room are doing something of the sort.' She contemplated Dolly with the hopelessness of an inventor whose model has failed to comply with his plans. 'Only for you, of course, it would have to be deadly serious.'

'What do you suggest?' asked Dolly, rather too obviously entering into the spirit of the thing.

'Oh, I don't know.' Elvire dabbed at the air with plump,

jewel-embossed hands. 'You might find a young man – hardly more than a boy – and educate him, get him to fall in love with you, break his heart, that kind of flim-flam. Scenes of parting – "can't live without you" – you could probably contrive to avoid the obligatory Night together – then I play the false friend who so considerately telegraphs to Calixte – something not too specific, so that he never actually suspects – boy shoots himself, maybe – Calixte, ever so solicitous, asks: "Why are you crying?" and you say: "Oh, it's nothing really" – curtain, applause, public delirious, critics wild, a run at the Variétés for the next decade. Too melodramatic? Don't stare at the waiter, he'll start getting interested in me again. Waiters are detestable. Don't have an affair with a waiter.'

It wasn't the waiter Dolly was looking at, but she wouldn't tell Elvire that. She was beginning to wonder whether, indeed, she would tell her anything significant again.

She did not go straight to her room. Something contagious held on to her in the restless atmosphere of the hotel foyer, where, late as it was, people loitered and chatted as if waiting for something to take place without which their day was not complete. The orchestra was in full career and a card party was going at canasta in a mood of almost hysterical conten-tiousness. With their sinuous turns of the waist and shoulders, satirising the abundant lack of grace in the movements of those they attended, the Splendide's servants, their faces satur-nine yet always faintly contemptuous, hovered and whirled among the scatter of guests and luggage, nonchalant per-formers in a mime of limitless competence.

Smiling, unoppressed by her solitude, Dolly found herself in a corner of the writing room and ordered a cocktail. Though Elvire's formula for amusement had seemed banal to the point of coarseness, she could hardly deny herself the pleasure of imagining, at least, the possibilities held out by her present situation. She had pointedly refused the invitation to go to

Annecy, not just because her friend's manner of delivering it was so irksome, but because she had suddenly grasped the value of being left entirely alone. The cherished assumption that rich people are stupid and resourceless would neither have pleased nor suited her. However loudly she might complain to Calixte, she could always find something to enjoy, even without him.

He was not to be told of Elvire's dereliction. Between thoughtful sips of her cocktail, Dolly decided that though she wasn't going to lie to her husband, she would volunteer only the most general information. Swearing Elvire and Freddy to silence smacked of vulgar conspiracy: she felt she could comfortably assume, however, that they would at least produce an impression of having spent the week looking after her, if only to remain in Calixte's good graces.

She finished her cocktail with the sardonic reflection that drinking on her own must have besmirched her character irredeemably in the eyes of the hotel. She was grateful that, easy prey though she now was, nobody had sat down beside her and started to make himself troublesome. It was midnight and life was still hectically in evidence around her as she entered the lift, alone except for the spotty-faced attendant who turned the handle and pulled back the grille. His 'goodnight, madame' as she stepped out into the corridor nettled her somewhat. It seemed to hint at bedtime, a little head on the pillow and sweet dreams, all of which were odious whether in form or conception. She had never presumed to wish sweet dreams to Calixte. Some of his, she knew, were very odd indeed.

The cage swung aloft and Dolly was left alone in the corridor. Its circumscribed emptiness, dimly lit and dead to any reverberation, was suddenly rather frightening. She fumbled nervously with her key and, once inside her sitting room, took care to lock the door. Nevertheless she hurried at once to throw open the balcony windows for the sake, as much as anything else, of the noises from the town below and the snatches of music still wafting up from the dining room. Kicking off her shoes, she remembered, as she had had to remember several times that day, the absence of Victorine, and promptly picked them up and carried them through into the bedroom. The action brought to her a sudden, almost anarchic awareness of her own liberty, the more acute since she was conscious also of how soon it was likely to end.

She stretched herself out on the sofa, opened the newspaper Calixte had bought but forgotten to take with him, and began to read a notice of the Tsar and Tsarina of Russia's visit to their villa in the Crimea. 'Their Imperial Majesties are attended by numerous officials of the court, Marshal Count Benckendorff, Prince Gagarin, Prince Obolensky (Chief of the Imperial Cabinet), Princess Galitzine (Mistress of the Robes), Count Rostovtzoff, Countess Golenichev Kutuzov (lady-in-waiting), etcetera'. How dire that 'etcetera' sounded! Wherever the Imperial Majesties went, there would always be an etcetera or two, or five, or sixteen, or a hundred and fifty, to trouble their solitariness. Dolly, not in the least envious, decided she would have a bath, get into bed and speculate thereafter on the likelihood of anybody really enjoying themselves under the guardianship of chamberlains and waiting-women. Feeling the weight of her necklace and wondering why she hadn't taken it off earlier, she got up, opened the boudoir door and found a young man sitting in front of the dressing-table mirror.

'Just wait a minute or two till I've fixed this earring,' he said, without turning round, while Dolly stood transfixed with amazement, watching his reflection in the glass. His coolness, since she was totally unprepared for it, checked whatever conventional impulses she might have had to scream or send for the police.

'There!' The young man turned round in the manner of someone concerned to create an effect. 'Seriously now, how do you think that looks?'

He was not much more than twenty, with a thin, white

face, eyes full of alertness, and a sharp nose and chin. It was not clear to Dolly whether she was supposed to comment seriously on the effect created by the ensemble of his shabby evening clothes and her garnet necklace and earrings, but she was able with honesty to tell him that red was somehow inappropriate.

'Oh, do you really think so? What a pity! I thought they'd go nicely with the black and white. Colours are so important, don't you find?'

'Yes,' she murmured half-heartedly, beginning to wonder if he actually existed. 'I imagine you couldn't manage the rings as well.'

He laughed, as though taking for granted her under-standing of the incidental problems entailed. 'Not for want of trying, but in my business one's got to have hands like bunches of carrots.'

Resentful of having to put such a blatant question, Dolly nonetheless forced herself to enquire what his business was. She wished he'd stop staring at her. His scrutiny was not at all flattering.

'I'm an acrobat,' he said, 'of sorts. That's to say, I do some clowning as well. I had an act with a chum, but we quarrelled yesterday and he went down south to a circus he knows of.'

She was absolutely not going to ask him what he was doing at Aix-les-Bains. It was all she could do to ask him, for that matter, what he was doing in front of her dressing-table mirror. He went on looking at her steadfastly, his eyes full of expectant laughter, so that she had to turn her face away to avoid laughing herself. It suddenly occurred to her that she was not in the least afraid. Her mind was far more busily exercised in trying to place him than in working out the orthodox processes which should lead to his arrest and even-tual conviction.

'You won't throw me out, will you?' he said, leaning back, thoroughly relaxed, against the dressing-table.

'I'm taking it for granted that you'll leave when I ask you

17

to do so,' rejoined Dolly crisply. 'Is there somewhere you can go to?'

His face – and she was growing steadily more preoccupied with it as a face – assumed an expression of mock outrage.

'My dear, I've got a room. It isn't especially good as rooms go, but it's near the station.'

'I don't think I especially like you calling me your dear.'

'Why? Because it makes you feel less powerful?' He smiled a colossal smile, slung across his face like a hammock, which made her garnet drops quiver on his ears. Dolly began to have an idea, so bizarre in its general outline that one part of her wondered where it could possibly have arrived from.

'You never thought that my husband might find you, I suppose.'

'I saw you saying goodbye to him this morning. That's why it's convenient to live close to the station.'

She shivered, and when the young man drew a silver brooch from his pocket saying 'Yours, no?' she clasped both hands to her mouth in genuine fear.

'You dropped it yesterday in the Villa des Fleurs, and then I couldn't find you to give it back.'

He held it out to her in his large hands. Dolly paused before taking the brooch from him, as if it had been a scorpion he was offering. She stared at it for a moment, feeling him watching her. Then, in what she presumed to be her best tones of chilly detachment, she said: 'I presume you know I could ask them to send for the police.'

The young man shrugged. 'I'm in your power, if you want it to be that simple.'

His insouciance was beginning to make Dolly cross. It was time to put her idea into execution. 'Get up,' she said. Rather to her surprise, he did so at once. 'Take those boxes next to the wardrobe and put them on the sofa.' She went out of the bourdoir ahead of him and stood strategically close to the bedroom door. Obediently he placed the two dress boxes and the shoes on one side of the sofa.

'Now' she said, as curtly as she knew how, 'remove your clothes.'

Betraying no surprise, the young man started to undress. She watched him with an increasing sense that she had begun a process both obscure and irreversible. His movements, in taking off his shoes and socks, folding his trousers and unfastening his shirt-studs, were swift, neat and professional – as of course, she reflected, they would be if he honestly was an acrobat and accustomed to rapid changes of clothing. Her scrutiny clearly didn't embarrass him. When it became obvious that he was going to take off his vest and drawers as well and stand naked before her, she said hurriedly: 'You can stop now.'

In this state he appeared neither male nor female. She ought to have taken his robust muscularity for granted, but the consistently epicene quality of his gestures and expressions belied this. His reserves of secret amusement as he stood, hands on hips, awaiting further instructions were seemingly limitless.

'Open one of those boxes,' said Dolly, striving to maintain the deliberately flavourless tone of her earlier instructions, 'and put on the dress you'll find there.'

He pulled back the lid, picked up the dress and shook it out appraisingly. Then, without the least demur, he scrambled deftly in.

'You could come and hook me up. I can do it myself, but it's always nicer if you've got someone to do it for you.'

Silently Dolly hooked up the back of the dress, in wry consideration that she had done the same thing for herself earlier tonight, in the absence of Victorine.

'The shoes?'

She nodded. With no obvious effort he slid his bare feet into the first pair. As he did so, she found herself noticing that the hands he had described as bunches of carrots were in reality small and almost powerless in their appearance.

'Now walk into the boudoir, turn round and come back again. Slowly. And leave the door wide open.'

The young man stood up and moved serenely towards the boudoir. Dolly had not necessarily expected him to be altogether lacking in grace, but she was entirely taken aback by the confidence with which he executed her commands. In the conviction of his assumed femininity there was an alarming naturalness. She wondered how many times he had done this before. Pausing before the mirror he surveyed himself academically.

'*Mousseline de soie.*'

'What?'

'This dress. Pretty patterns on the sleeves. These shoes are too wide-fitting for a woman. Your husband didn't order them, did he?'

'You've no right to suggest . . .'

'I know, but he might have done. You can't tell with husbands.'

He swept back into the room and came very close to her.

'I'm going to kiss you,' he said. She gave no sign of reluctance. It felt like a niece kissing her aunt, the religious niece, maybe, about whom she had joked with Elvire but whom the dress now became in so emphatically worldly a fashion.

'Tomorrow', she said, 'we'll find you a hat.'

Another huge smile slung itself between his ears. 'A parasol would be nice too.'

As silently as before, Dolly unhooked the dress and hung it in the wardrobe while the young man got back into his clothes. He handed her the garnet necklace and earrings as though entrusting them to her for safekeeping. 'At what time tomorrow?'

'Noon. Walk up the stairs, don't use the lift, they'll only be curious about you.'

He nodded, silently opened the door and slipped out into the corridor. A moment later he was back, laughing richly but noiselessly to himself, to say: 'They call me Toto, but it's really Antoine. I don't care what you call me,' and was gone again.

For a long time Dolly stood with her back against the door, hearing the laughter and music still drifting up from the terrace below, but unable any longer to relate these sounds to her experience. When she caught sight of her own face staring at her from the mirror on the wall by the door into the bathroom, she wondered whose it was, just as she wondered where she had come across Calixte's umbrella, which he had neglected to take with him and which now stood propped beside the table like some object of long-forgotten ritual significance. If he telephoned now she might not know him.

The telephone preserved an obdurate silence. Suddenly released from passivity she went into the bathroom, turned on the taps and threw a handful of salts into the tub. Then she began undressing. Again she stared abstractedly at herself in the glass, putting both hands to her face and smoothing back her hair. She laughed.

'I can't possibly bring myself to call him Toto,' she said.

She was still wondering whether there was anything notice-ably odd about her when Elvire and Freddy called at the hotel next morning. It was all she could do not to ask them directly. The motor stood spluttering at the foot of the steps, and Elvire, sounding rather half-hearted, said: 'You're absolutely sure you don't want to come with us?'

'I shall be quite safe,' answered Dolly.

Elvire giggled. 'That's wasn't what I asked.'

'What are you going to tell Calixte?' enquired Freddy, with the obvious motive of ensuring that Dolly would not betray their desertion.

'That I went to bed early and read books. If necessary I'll tell him that I wouldn't go with you.' She smiled. 'But I'm sure it won't come to that.'

Elvire kissed her with a faintly roguish complicity. The pair got into the car.

'What are you going to do with those dresses?' Elvire called out as Freddy started the engine.

'I thought I'd keep them,' Dolly said, 'to give as presents. They must look good on somebody or other.'

Standing at the top of the steps waving as they drove off, she was reminded of a story she had read as a child in which a heroic princess, in a city threatened with enemy attack, had refused an ally's offer of safety and watched steadfastly as the last refugees fled without her. Dolly, feeling vulnerable rather than heroic, retreated to her room and fretted over the *Magazin des Modes* until Antoine should come.

Starting to her feet at the sound of his knock, she realised how much she must have longed for him to arrive. Now, however, he was unrecognisable to her. The only thing she recalled from last night was his long hair, swept back in a brown mane across the collar of his crumpled linen jacket. Otherwise the intense, livid whiteness of his skin, his narrow, purplis lips and the slightly mocking somnolence of his drooping eyelids were features she had either forgotten or else wholly failed to absorb. He appeared older now and even more self-possessed than before, as if an entire plan had taken shape which he was bent upon putting into immediate execution. Under his arm was a small parcel. Having kissed Dolly perfunctorily, he chucked it on to the sofa.

'Stockings,' he said, 'we forgot.'

She gaped. 'Do you mean that you bought them?'

'Of course. I could have worn my performance tights, but they'd have been rather uncomfortable in this weather. I haven't got much money left. Still, it was worth the expense, don't you think?' His glance assumed an unusual seriousness. 'You're absolutely to promise, by the way, not to give me anything. Not that I'll ask, but it will spoil things if you do. I don't want to be grateful to you.'

'Yes, I see,' said Dolly vaguely. She was still thinking about the stockings. Could he really have walked into a shop and asked for a pair of women's stockings, perhaps even demurring as to their size or colour? The curious decorum that now seemed to govern them forbade her to do more than silently ponder the question.

'Today . . .' he began enthusiastically.

'Today?'

'That brown one with those ridiculous flowers, I think. And you said you'd find me a hat.'

He was – wasn't he? – commanding her, but almost without thinking she went into the boudoir and brought out the correct box. In the precise, orderly fashion of the previous night Antoine began to undress, laying carefully aside the drab jacket, waistcoat and trousers which seemed to have been chosen with an eye to their flagrant anonymity. Dolly realised that he knew she was watching him, yet the exercise was now so absorbing that she could scarcely take her eyes off the figure in front of her. His body, as he tackled the various processes of unbuttoning, folding and doffing, had a peculiar denial of form to it which reminded her of a trick she had been shown as a child, whereby an ordinary glove could be transformed into numberless human and animal shapes simply by pulling the fingers in. She would honestly not have been surprised to see the protean creature before her grow additional arms and legs had he needed to do so.

As he sat on the edge of the bed, rolling the stockings over his knees in a no-nonsense manner and then producing, as if out of the air, the pair of elastic garters which were to hold them in place, she suddenly said: 'Léopoldina, it's Léopoldina, no?'

Antoine smiled without looking up. Clearly it was a conclusion at which he had waited for her to arrive.

'Ah, you've seen it?'

'Yes, twice. Calixte enjoys that kind of thing.'

He laughed. 'I like "that kind of thing". Do you enjoy "that kind of thing", as well?'

'To be perfectly candid, I thought you were a bit sinister. When your partner came on first, the one who does the catching, I thought we were merely going to see some conventional acrobatic display, but then . . .'

'My appearance outraged you, was that it?' He looked as if he hoped so.

'No, it was the way you seemed to alter whenever you moved from one thing to another. You were never the same person for more than a minute or two.'

'Goodness, you're perceptive. I suppose it never occurred to you that this was how I intended it?'

Dolly bridled, 'Does one go to the music hall to consider the motives of the performers? That blond wig, by the way, was ridiculous.'

Antoine, grinning ferociously, stood up off the bed. 'You say that simply because you know what I look like with it off. Would you have preferred me with my own hair?'

'Why not? I imagine that's why you grew it long.'

'Not necessarily. Now the dress. This one is a fright, isn't it? But I'll give it a touch of character. I imagine you wouldn't be seen dead in this sort of dress.'

She had failed once again to make him angry and realised it was only his imperturbability which had made her try in the first place. His last remark, in any case, was irresistible. Without waiting to be asked, she began doing up the buttons at the back. She felt like a mother dressing a child for a party, and when she said 'Now turn round' the illusion was complete. It didn't matter much that there was no bust to speak of. He had begun, in a manner which more enchanted than disturbed her, not to look like a man.

A pair of conspirators, they decided with eager haste upon what to do about his hair, and on top of the finished effect, created by a strategic pinning or two, Dolly pinned a hat with a veil. She stood back to contemplate the result. Antoine went and tweaked at his dress in front of the glass.

'Not bad,' he declared, 'but we'll improve on it in time.'

'In time,' she echoed, and they both laughed as though the words freed something between them. 'Now we'll go to the Casino. Maybe you'll find something else I've lost.'

'Stop being so significant. Do you want me to put my veil down?'

'If it suits you.'

He shrugged, seeming to imply that it was more a matter of what suited her, and pulled down the veil. As he walked across the room, it struck Dolly that she had never seen it done better. She wanted to applaud, but a certain gravity in his manner restrained her.

Together, in a silent mutual compliance like the gradual formulation of a private discourse, they slipped along the corridor, the two of them, and waited for the arrival of the lift. Dolly felt an absurd thrill of apprehension as she heard the clanking of the machinery and the cage swung into view. To the spotty-faced lift-boy she was inclined to attribute extraordinary perceptions, a judgement based on the groundless assumption that, since he saw everyone going up and down each day, he must somehow have a truer notion of them, in the austere rectangle where, for a brief moment, he held them captive, than could be gained in the ordinary confines of social intercourse. She shivered at the thought that Antoine might break the silence, but he remained absolutely still while they lurched slowly earthwards, a figure dehumanised in curious magnificence under the dark folds of his veil.

She had another tremulous minute or two when a taxi was called for her from the hotel steps. Would he know how to get into the car, what to do with the folds of his skirt or how to take the hand proffered by the doorman? She need not have worried. The whole manoeuvre passed off with a consummate naturalness which made her long to know whether this too had been a part of Léopoldina's act. Now, however, was not the moment to ask. That sense of decorum, of appropriate times and gestures, voices and expressions, which Calixte so admired in her, had seldom seemed more necessary if the adventure in hand was to be properly controlled.

They sauntered through the Casino and drank iced tea, they made a methodical inspection of the shops in rue Macaire and lingered pleasurably over luncheon. Only when they were sitting in the Jardin Anglais did it begin to occur to Dolly that she had become attuned to the sound of Antoine's voice without even pausing to consider whether it was noticeably a man's. Yet she was not happy. Or rather, as she might more conscientiously have expressed it, still she was not happy. Antoine discerned this almost as soon as they sat down.

'Why are you looking so cross? You haven't looked cross since last night.'

For a while she didn't answer, not through any reluctance but because it was impossible to say exactly what she felt without laboriously turning everything over first of all, like trying to get at something in the back of a cupboard. Then, not without effort, she said: 'It's . . . it's because of you.'

'I hardly supposed otherwise.'

'Oh, stop being so flippant! Men are always making fun of serious things.'

The hammock smile spread across his face. 'I'm still a man, then?'

'No you're not, no, that's what I don't like.'

'What exactly?'

Clenching her fists to stop herself from shrieking, Dolly hissed: 'Because you're not embarrassed enough. In fact you're not embarrassed at all. I expected you at least to fall over on the Casino steps, but oh no, you must do it perfectly.'

'What did I do best? Go on, was there something which really flabbergasted you?'

Her anger left him unconcerned. She needed to get even with his professionalism.

'It was when you were looking at handkerchiefs in the shop. I thought something shameful was going to happen.'

'You hoped it was.'

'That's unfair.'

'I'm sorry, you're quite right, it was stupid of me. Please go on.'

His serenity continued to be outrageous. In a slightly quavering tone she resumed: 'You asked to see men's handkerchiefs. You told them you were choosing for a man and had a little laugh about it with the shopgirl. She was looking at you all the time and never suspected, I could see that.'

'And you,' he pursued, 'what did you feel?'

'When?'

'When I was looking at handkerchiefs. Were you jealous?'

In answer Dolly got up and walked a little way along the path. She had indeed been jealous, but of the girl behind the counter, whose forwardness with Antoine had seemed quite uncalled for, but she wasn't going to admit that now. In terms of the feelings she had to invest in it, the contrivance was becoming grotesquely laboured. She turned to watch Antoine coming after her, a tall *jolie laide* in a brown velvet hat, who gave the beige tussore horror a paradoxical elegance. She felt as if she had invented him, and the spectacle made her helpless and afraid. What on earth was she to do? He was horrifyingly near her in all the perfection of his disguise.

Under the lowered parasol he whispered: 'On the way back to the hotel can we buy some chocolates?'

She bit her lip and answered ungraciously enough: 'I thought you said you weren't going to ask me for anything. What sort?'

'The Italian ones, that taste of nuts but don't actually have them in the filling. I'm fond of those.'

'I suppose I've got to make you a present of them.' Dolly stared resentfully up at him, wondering when she would actually start to detest his remorseless candour.

'Until I get some money, yes. I don't intend to live off you. I always pay back what I borrow. Renaud was the one who used to fritter it. He sponged like the devil. The little swine still owes me twenty francs. I'll get it off him, I'm mean that way.'

They came out into the Place du Revard. Its openness made Dolly nervous. She half expected to see Freddy and Elvire waiting for her on the steps of the Lamartine and Calixte to come sauntering up from the station.

'We're getting a cab,' she announced. 'I'll tell it to stop at that shop near the hotel, and we can ask for your chocolates there.'

'You're really not enjoying this, are you?' said Antoine.

Without answering, she almost pushed him inside the motor, and they accomplished the chocolate-buying in an atmosphere of tight-lipped grimness. When the desk-clerk at the hotel handed her a letter and she read Victorine's starkly formal announcement that, owing to her mother's worsening condition, a return from Nantes was unlikely for at least ten days, Dolly felt a stab of irritation at the liberty implicitly granted to her.

Once they had gained the room and Antoine again asked: 'Well, are you enjoying it or not?' she wanted to scream with annoyance, but did nothing less dignified than sit on the edge of the sofa, clenching her hands and pressing her knees together.

'Look, we'll give it up,' he said. 'It's not working, you're not relaxed with me like I want you to be.'

She stared intently at the cushions as he came and sat down beside her. There was an immense, hard silence between the pair of them.

'Stop pitying me,' she said at length, 'I can hear you feeling sorry for me.'

His arm came round her. 'We needn't do it like this if you don't want to. There are other ways. I just thought it was fun, your idea.' He kissed her. She liked the dampness of his tongue in her mouth and the sleepy droop of his eyelids. Suffused with a sensual torpor which numbed her earlier crossness, she fell back against the edge of the sofa and heard the lawnmower going again outside. If they went on like this there would soon be no lawn to mow. A friend had told her about an alienist outside Paris who made his patients mow the lawn for a therapeutic exercise until there was only the earth left. Antoine sat up and began pulling the grips and switches out of his hair, smiling expectantly down at her as he did so. Suddenly she didn't feel like having to make a decision.

When she was a little girl, she and her sisters used to climb under the bedclothes whenever it thundered in the afternoon. They never devised an excuse for this that would convince the grownups, and in later years they never came to understand in themselves. Dolly could only recall it in terms of the obscure delight inspired by drawing the curtains and burrowing under the sheets as the thunder, hollow and pursuing, rolled towards them through the window.

She remembered it now as Antoine made love to her. His narrow body had lost that curious eel-like flexuousness assisting his earlier transformation from man to woman, and the spiky, starveling hardness of it could be felt through a skin white almost to transparency. His engrossed desire battened greedily on her indolence, and something close to anger seemed to fuel his clasp on her, the press and hurt of him, as if he were getting his own back, carrying out a long-delayed plan chewed in a bitter frustration like the morsel of belt or shoe-leather gnawed at by a castaway. She wanted to see his face when he came, but as soon as she put up a hand to turn his head towards her he winced away, burrowing into the crook of her neck and choking into the pillow as though the consummation had nothing to do with her.

It was different with Calixte. Calixte always used to look at her solemnly when they were together thus, drawing her within the unflinching, inclusive certainty of his gaze. It occurred to Dolly that she did not specially miss him. She would be glad of his return in a day or so, yet the innate realism which was always at odds with her luxuriant imagination made her search for guilt where little existed. That curious deadness to eventuality she had felt earlier was still there. Smiling to herself, she stroked the nape of the boy's neck under its tousled bunches of hair.

'Let's have some of those chocolates,' he murmured, 'the ones we bought earlier.' He had seemed almost asleep, yet bounced neatly from bed to sofa to grab the chocolates, tear the ribbon off the box and vault back into the clearing of bedclothes he had made beside her.

'Want one? These are the best ever, aren't they? They remind me of Turin.'

She had never been to Turin.

'We did a circus there once. I hate circuses. They smell. I mean, so do theatres, but at least it's a smell you know, like your own. This one was just about all right, I suppose. No wild beasts, only horses and a couple of girls doing things with spinning plates, some fellows got up like Indian jugglers, the high-wire acts and the three of us.'

'Three?'

'Yes.' He became old and knowing. 'You have to have the two catchers to do the warm-up. And they looked good, Théo and Bob, tights, sashes, spangles, you can imagine. Then I'd come on, all got up with ringlets and flounces like a bareback rider only I hadn't got a horse, do a number or two, and go into the act. I was Pepita in those days, Léopoldina came along when I got more classy.'

He lay back against her arm and began, between intervals of munching the truffles and licking the corners of his mouth, to resume his career in a way which Dolly found simultaneously fascinating and depressing. It didn't matter that her interest in the details, the number and styles of his dresses, the differences between the contract at the Parisiana and the contract at the Eldorado, the clown who had wanted to marry him, the Brazilian who had offered to be his protector, was more polite than enthusiastic. He wasn't, she realised, doing this for her, but to resolve something within himself, and it was this newly disclosed perspective of doubt, adumbrating as it so potently seemed to do his entire approach to their swiftly accomplished intimacy, which began to absorb her.

At the same time the impulse towards tenderness aroused by Antoine's singularity opened the earliest of passages to gloom. Dolly could see, by its very nature as a haphazard game, pleasing one moment, embarrassing the next, what their bizarre liaison might become and, dreading an access of something like affection, took away the hand with which she had been abstractedly caressing him.

He noticed it and murmured: 'Don't stop, it's nice when you do that,' and of course she knew, even as her fingers touched his lean, wiry arm, that she would have to go on, would have to let him turn as he did now, his face against her breasts, still muttering about Renaud and what a stingy little shyster he'd been and how he'd loused up the act good and proper, would have at last to see him as something more like a threat than a diversion. the memory of what she had felt earlier, when they were out together in the town, came back to make her shiver.

There was one thing she could not understand. She wanted to know why, all the time he was present, her curiosity about him seemed to dwindle to nothing, as if she knew everything about him, whereas when he was not with her she felt devoured by an obsessive eagerness to pry into the most trifling details of his existence. She wondered how on earth she had kept herself from asking what means he had used to get into her room in the first place. She'd still not found out where he was staying, why he had come to Aix and what had been the occasion of the quarrel with his friend Renaud.

Yet the conditions which determined, and went on determining, her ignorance held their own logic. Something about Antoine annihilated the past. He neither possessed nor needed any perspective, and given what she suspected of her incipient feelings towards him, Dolly was unwilling to accord one. She could still find a refuge in her singular capacity for detached speculation, which made it so odd that she should passively accept him thus, a being with shades but no shadows, whose dimensions seemed constantly to be reassembling themselves in an unexpected form.

Beside him she felt dimly ordinary in preserving a definite context. To be the daughter of a newspaper proprietor, with two brothers in the army, to have been educated by the Ursulines at Ponitoise, married for five years to Calixte, his father's partner in a chain of cotton mills, with a house in Passy and a villa at Etretat – in the unyielding absoluteness of such facts lay a damning banality.

When she contemplated Antoine the next day it was with a frankly acknowledged envy. Her earlier anger and bewilderment had gone, leaving only a distilled admiration that was almost awe as he renewed the total illusion while entirely altering the terms of the performance. Yesterday he had been the diffident veiled companion, moving with tentative grace beside her. Now he assumed another character, knowing, subtly flirtatious, conveying a liveliness in the movement of head and hands which extinguished altogether the recollection of the dignified Racinian confidante he had been at first. Though careful to avoid talking, save when necessary, he had modulated his voice for the part. Dolly knew she was never going to ask him how it was done, but this, above all his other tricks, she longed to know the secret of.

As they paraded through the Villa des Fleurs she began to catch the infection of the boy's sheer delight in bringing off everything so brilliantly. She felt like flaunting him in all his wondrous singularity, as if he had been captured in some land unknown to cartographers and sent to her as a present with a train of ambassadors in tow. When she bought him chocolates, the box was a veritable reward.

Now he was eating them in her bed again, his clothes sloughed across the carpet and the familiar angles of him sprawled comfortably across her.

'I had a telephone call this morning,' Dolly announced apropos of nothing in particular, 'from my husband. He said he'd be back the day after tomorrow.'

Antoine grinned. 'He'd better be.'

'What is that supposed to mean?'

'Whatever it means. If he came back now what would you do?' He bit the end off another truffle. 'You can give me a year's supply of these. That was a stupid question, by the way, you needn't answer it. What I really wanted to . . .' He paused and looked up at her, all bravado drained from him, only a kind of boyish desperation left, a pleading for something he had to know. 'Have you . . . were you ever unfaithful to him before?'

Dolly burst out laughing. 'In unimportant ways, I don't remember.'

'Why is that funny?'

'Because you wanted to be the first. But there never is a first, there's always been somebody else, the person who hasn't asked the question.' Glumly she stared at the little white heap of his singlet by the leg of the sofa. 'For half a second yesterday I wondered if I was the first for you, and of course I wasn't. Don't ask me to tell you about them, they weren't in the least bit interesting.'

Antoine was silent, sitting up on his elbow, his shoulders hunched. Then, clenching her furiously to him, he muttered: 'I want you to take me to the Pavillon this evening. I want you to pay for me. I promise I'll make it good.'

Dolly smiled. 'You couldn't very well do it for yourself, could you?' Then she realised, when she saw him still frowning, that she had better take him seriously after all.

When the light came up and they stepped into its cube of garish light, Antoine was more thoroughly unrecognisable to her than ever. The bones in his face seemed to have rearranged themselves so as to convey an air of patrician reserve, an elongated, hollow-cheeked scorn, a odd deadness in the eyes, repelling any attempt at conversation. It became obvious that he had decided carefully who at this moment he was going to be and that in this absolute alteration of character from the bold, confident creature she had taken out earlier Dolly was meant to read a warning. There was a distinct awe in the lift-boy's manner as he opened the doors for them. The sense of it made her heart sink. She didn't want to leave the hotel, she never wanted to leave it, she wanted to hide within the promise of safety vouchsafed by its order and ritual. She hated the way the commissionaire smiled at her when he opened the door of the taxi, as though he had been sending her to execution. She wanted to be back in her room with Antoine warm and smooth and sinewy against her, eating chocolates, not as he was now, perched upright, a silent, imperious dowager sailing towards dinner.

Over the meal itself he was insufferable. A frost seemed to form around him and spread to the waiters, who got correspondingly nervous and over-attentive. The few words he uttered might have shaped themselves in vapour for all the warmth they conveyed. Dolly's attempts at provoking him into speech were quite useless, and she realised that beneath his apparent detachment he was meditating something which merely awaited an appropriate moment to declare itself. Yet even as she shrank from the desire to know, she ackowledged the depth of his allure. Had he left her now she would have wept with rage and frustration. Though she hated the limits Antoine had imposed on his compliance, it appeared, in the space of a mere three days, to have altered her so that she would almost not have known herself.

Calixte's return would solve nothing. Briefly Dolly had imagined him as a saviour to whom she would cling with guilty fervour and beg him never to leave her like that again, after which, as she conceived it, some sort of contrition would then have to be endured in a general sense of her husband's solid, unspectacular virtues. But it wouldn't be like that, of course, precisely because of what there was to miss in

Antoine, the feel of his hair bunched coarse and luxuriant between her fingers, the deeply incised creases breaking on either side of his mouth like parentheses around his smile, the furrow in his back, the curious knots of muscle gathering and disappearing on his shoulders and thighs, his restlessness, loquacity and self-absorption, and above all his eagerness for her which in itself was not so much a longing or a devotion as the most selfish kind of hunger, as though she were merely necessary to his survival.

Never for a moment had she considered the possibility of a relationship which offered so little room for flattery. Those two flings she had teasingly mentioned to Antoine were each based on a presumption, if not an absolute certainty, that the motive force in either case was her own attractiveness at a given moment. With him, however, this was not even vaguely suggested. He'd never itemised her beauty, still less made vague allusions to it, though clearly it was not her money, her taste in dress or even, as she now sardonically reflected, her jewels which originally drew him to her. She found herself longing for the merest seasoning of compliment, for the most trifling demonstration of gallantry, and despised herself profoundly for such common desires. It was as if, within their very short intimacy, they had gained the acidulated familiarity of seasoned lovers on the verge of a mutual rejection. Suddenly she saw herself as horrifyingly sophisticated. At this rate she would be calling him Toto.

Aware now that he had hardly eaten anything, she paid the bill with a little tea-tasting noise of irritation and saw him stare accusingly at her, as if to ask what all that was meant to mean. They got up and walked in silence through the restaurant, she following him like an obedient paid companion. The night breeze, laden with suggestions and excitements on which she could not lay hold, made her feel confined and awkward. In its little alcove behind a clump of potted palms, the orchestra sliced away at tango music, and a party of diners was laughing so loudly that their table threatened to rise into the air.

She felt lonely enough to telephone Calixte when she got back to the hotel. He was still, said a voice, at the factory. It was a quarter past eleven. A spurt of irrational anger made her believe he had done it on purpose, that he knew she wanted him to be there, all the appetising substance and integrity of him established by the solicitous tone he used when talking to her, as if she was an invalid and he her doctor. Then, turning, she saw Antoine, as haughtily reserved as before, waiting for her at the lift entrance, and of course it was somehow to be his fault that Calixte had not been there.

Silently they went up together. As she locked the door of her sitting room, Dolly was afraid. Antoine had walked to the window and stood with his back to her. She was afraid that if he turned round, the face she saw would not be his, yet foolhardily she said: 'Don't stand so near the window or people will see you.'

In a movement that suddenly belied all his earlier assumed femininity, he put his arms up and grasped the curtains, not to draw them but to hang from them exhausted. Then he turned, his eyes more sombrely preoccupied than she had yet seen them, and wrenched off his hairpieces as if he did not know what on earth they were.

'Why don't you speak to me?' he said.

The flagrant injustice made her cry out. 'You! You don't speak to me!'

But he wasn't having any of that. Savagely he snatched at her arm. 'Nevertheless you don't speak to me. Not as you ought. Anyone would think it was a game.'

'It is,' said Dolly sternly, 'It's what I wanted. I wanted to play with you. You seemed . . .' she shrugged, finishing, weakly, 'as if you'd like to play.'

This clearly staggered him. He peered at her, narrowing his eyes suspiciously. 'You admit it?'

'Admission doesn't come into it. I might just as well enquire why you went along with the whole thing in the first place. Don't tell me you haven't enjoyed it.'

Antoine stared at the ground and murmured: 'It wasn't that kind of enjoyment I was after.'

If this was an insult, Dolly felt she had a right to be offended.

'I suppose not. You were apparently in search of my jewellery. I should have rung the bell at once and make a scene. You'd probably have liked that, with my emeralds dangling off your ears.'

'You haven't got any emeralds.'

'Yes I have, I just haven't shown you them.'

'Anyway, it was garnets.'

'What?' She had not been concentrating. Instead she thought how incredibly young the evening dress made him look once he took off his hairpieces. He looked like a girl at her first dance.

'Garnets,' he repeated irritably, 'I was wearing your garnet necklace.'

He stared at her with a brooding frown which suggested that she formed some part of a plan whose components had suddenly failed to function quite as intended.

'You don't remember, do you?' he said. 'It's been three days and you don't remember.'

He is starting to annoy me, she thought, and he hasn't done that before.

'Do stop repeating yourself. And don't keep picking me up on everything I say. And do get out of that dress, you look utterly ridiculous in it.'

Even as she said this, she knew it had hurt him. Perhaps it was meant to wound. He flinched away from her, for the first time angular and graceless, his mouth twitching so that she thought he was going to cry.

'You don't know,' he said breathlessly, and hung upon the curtains with his back to her as he had done before, staring out into the night. Turning again, he looked tired to the point where every resource had been used up. His hands stretched out pleadingly towards her.

'I would have gone if you'd asked me, but you never did. There was a feeling I had that you knew I'd been watching you, you knew I was in the restaurant when you had dinner with your friend, the one with red hair.'

'Elvire,' she murmured automatically.

'Anyway, you can always say I took advantage of you.' Putting his arms behind him, Antoine started deftly to unhook the dress. 'Which I meant to. I'm glad I did.' He wriggled free and kicked off his shoes. Standing back on his heels, clad only in crumpled petticoats, he had the appearance of an African in ritual costume. Dolly suddenly felt that to see him naked would disgust her, and was relieved when he suddenly sat down, with every sign of weariness, on the bed and threw himself back on his elbows. The music and chatter from the terrace below had stopped and the enfolding silence was almost comforting.

'Were you really in the restaurant?' Dolly said.

'Yes. I just walked in and pretended to look for someone. I'd watched you several times before that. I wanted to see how you did things, how you walked up the steps, what you did with your cloak, how you bent down to pick something up. When you dropped that brooch in the Villa des Fleurs, I wanted to give it back to you at once, just to see what you'd do, how you'd stretch out your hand to take it from me. But you'd gone by the time I'd got hold of it.'

'I see,' said Dolly with a touch of disappointment; 'it was an academic interest.'

Antoine stared at the boudoir door ahead of him. 'You don't really see. You can't believe I'm serious about anything, because you haven't any seriousness yourself. Maybe you had once, but it's gone. I don't mind that, you can always learn it again, there's plenty of time.'

It was the first thing he had said that evening which genuinely alarmed her. The phrase 'there's plenty of time' seemedly suddenly to illuminate, in the most lurid fashion, the essential difference between them both, a difference Dolly had suspected from the beginning but which, in the selective hold on reality she was learning to exert, had been pushed carefully to one side.

In a way which she imagined must make the meaning clear, she said: 'When my husband comes back, do you still want to go on seeing me?'

For answer, he flung himself further over the bed, so that his head and arms were hanging almost out of sight and she was left communicating with the rise and fall of his diaphragm above the crumpled petticoat.

'I don't know what you mean by "seeing" you. How would I see you anyway? That isn't the point.'

He sat up again, the perpetual restlessness in his face deepening, and hugged his knees up under his chin. Dolly was still standing beside the bed, wondering whether or not to sit down and realising that the more time she spent in wondering, the less likely she would be to sit down. Then he turned, his glance brightened by the sudden perception with which he prepared to confront her.

'I know what it is,' he said, pausing to smack his long, narrow lips together. 'It's that there's something inherently vulgar in you. Perhaps I don't mean vulgar, just commonplace. Everything you do, all your little suppositions and anticipations have a staleness about them. What on earth did you think I was? Maybe some wretched tart of a boy who'd spent all his life dressing up as Léopoldina and jumping through hoops on the music halls. Well I'm not, you know. My father's a doctor at Saumur, and I was at the Ecole Polytechnique for a year. They were going to make an engineer out of me. You never thought of that, did you?'

'Not exactly,' answered Dolly, furious yet determined not to let him have it all his own way.

'You worry about things like losing your brooch and

whether your maid's going to come back or not. And thought it'd be nice . . .' – his contempt sported with the word – 'nice to have some fun with me. I take back what I said about learning to be serious. You couldn't if you tried.'

A silent rage at him made her feel almost blind. If she could have seen clearly enough to pick up the bedside lamp, she would have used its metal base to beat his skull in. For her own sake, not for his, she drew away towards the boudoir door. She wanted to shout, to have servants clatter down the corridor, to wake up the entire hotel, to make such a row as would finish them both. Instead she heard herself muttering in a strange, disembodied growl, a voice produced by ventriloquism, by an oracle or a medium, but not hers: 'I hate your beastly professionalism. I hate the way you have to get everything just right. When you bought those stockings, I imagined it was simply because you'd decided to humour me, that you were entering into the spirit.'

'Why the deuce should I try to humour you? What good would that have done?'

'I don't know, it's what I thought. But instead you were being professional. No doubt you would have worried if there were holes in them.'

'Bang right I would. And bought new ones.' Antoine stared hard at her, his interest suddenly rekindled. 'You're sharp. Sometimes.'

'I merely guessed.'

'It doesn't matter, you're quite right. It's not a question of looking the part. Men can always look like women if they've a mind to. Have you noticed how hopeless women are at looking like men? Their bottoms are too big, of course, but that's a different matter.' He sat up, his face animated once more, and it was at this instant that Dolly most clearly understood the difference between his idea of reality and her own. What fired his imagination was theories, systems, calculations. He was able, she perceived, to transcend actuality because it bored him.

'The question is about being sincere,' he declared, 'or rather, being insincere. Ours is simply a different variety of humbug to yours. We can dress up, you can't. Yours is another sort of dishonesty, the kind that pretends it isn't there.'

'You make it seem so simple and obvious, but I still don't see what this has to do with buying stockings,' pursued Dolly inexorably.

'Ah, you wouldn't, would you?' Antoine retorted. 'I keep thinking you'll get there, but you don't.' Standing up, he stretched and yawned, then started to mooch about the room with his arms folded while Dolly watched him nervously. At length, fixing his gaze on the leg of an armchair, he said: 'In Paris they wanted to give me a show of my own. People liked the act. Poets came and saw it. One of them even wrote songs for me, but I never got to sing them. I didn't want any of that, not till I'd got everything right.' Suddenly his eyes engaged her again. 'Being a woman, that's it, you see. And you can't be a woman with holes in your stockings. When we went out tonight and I didn't eat anything, it wasn't because I didn't feel hungry. I just wanted to watch the women there. And I watched them, picking at their fish and their complete and sipping their half-glasses of wine and dancing and laughing and sulking and pretending to listen to men who bored them stupid and making those little smiles that mix hopelessness with complicity at the man on the opposite table. And I thought: "I can do all of this better than they do. They don't do it properly, they're not professional." I wanted to show them how to be a woman.'

Dolly laughed. 'And was that why you wouldn't speak to me?'

'Not just because of that.' He gave a little sigh, shrugged and slipped off the petticoat. Then, going to the wardrobe, he took out his evening clothes and slid into them with amazing despatch 'Well, I'm off,' he announced. 'I might be back tomorrow, so don't pack everything up. Oh, and I can ask them at the desk if your husband's back.'

Without another word he was gone. For a moment Dolly sat on the corner of the bed, staring as if entranced by the wrinkles and indentations his body had made while lying across it. Then she turned to look at the litter of clothes across the room, the petticoat like an empty bird's nest, the dress draped over the sofa arm with its sleeves spread out in supplication, the chemise cringing frightened in a corner and the two hairpieces tossed under the curtains. It was the kind of mess a fugitive makes, and he seemed to have fled from her. Yet he wasn't afraid, that she knew.

So far at least she had failed. Even if it was not obvious why, the clarity of his single perception scarcely alarmed her. The only frustration she felt was in being unable to articulate the sense of her failure to anybody else. Something demanded had not been given, some intimation he sought and couldn't find, and thus, with that strange capacity for swiftly abstracting himself from involvement with the urgency of a situation he had created, he simply left without any definite promise of returning.

Antoine's manner of parting gave Dolly no special cause for rancour. Her acceptance of it as characteristic made her more confident that she would see him again. She got up and started to fold the dress. She picked up the two hairpieces and put them into a dressing-table drawer. She tidied the chemise into a shelf of the wardrobe. When she took up the petticoat, a momentary impulse made her hold it close to her face before it too was put away. Suddenly she thought of Victorine and then remembered Calixte, if only to acknowledge that she had forgotten him. The two of them stood like distant watchers on the purlieus of her existence, its new immediacy defined by another presence altogether, to whose nature precaution, subterfuge and lying were alien and in whom, as she now perceived, there was no fear. And because

Dolly was unafraid, she too was starting to lose her earlier apprehensions.

Thus, she reasoned, he had jumped through paper hoops, slithered down ropes and swung from perch to perch on his trapezes, because the space between him and the sawdust floor or the planks of the stage was too insubstantial to matter. Perhaps that, after all, was what she most envied in him.

Getting ready for bed, Dolly glanced sardonically round the room. She looked at the chairs and tables, mirrors and cupboards, and realised that somebody's eye and sense of the fitness of things must have been responsible for assembling them in a fashion calculated not to disturb good taste but intended at the same time not to arrest the attention with too marked an individuality. The sheer half-heartedness of it all seemed contemptible, yet it had never struck her so forcibly before. Until now, indeed, it had never struck her at all. She began to wonder what on earth she was doing there.

In the morning she had a telephone call from Calixte. He asked her how she was and whether she had managed to amuse herself in his absence, to both of which questions she was able to offer rational answers. He would arrive tomorrow, he said, by the afternoon train from Paris. The warmth in his voice suggested that, for whatever reason, he was trying to encourage her, while at the same time magnificently not responding to her evident lack of enthusiasm. It made Dolly angry to think that if he found out about Antoine he would almost certainly forgive her. She wanted no more of that dreadful heroic calm.

She did not go out, but sat in her room in an absurd frenzy of expectation. It was years since anything similar had so overmastered her. After an hour or so of drumming her fingers on the chair-arm, pacing the length of the room, trying to concentrate for more than five lines on a magazine article and peering repeatedly from the balcony like Sister Anne in the tale of Bluebeard, she went downstairs and ate luncheon in miserable solitude.

They brought her a letter from Victorine, which she was certainly not going to read at table and put aside at once. Loneliness was no longer flattering. She became conscious that others in the dining room were watching her, with that critical stare which seemed to want to know what she might be doing on her own and lunching early. She began to see every gesture as measured and interpreted, each sip of water, each movement of knife and fork across the plate, as if the act of eating were being reviewed against the grid of a hard moral system. Having tried in vain with a second course, Dolly returned, vanquished to her room.

He was on her immediately, seizing her, pressing her head against the wall and gnawing at her with starved, furious kisses. She knew in that instant, as she clutched him to her and dug her fingers into the coarse mane of his hair, that she had meant to leave the door unlocked so that he would be there when she came in, for it to be like this between them. Staggering among the furniture like brawlers, they fumbled idiotically with buttons and laces, in a rage at each other's unget-at-able-ness, then she pushed him on to the bed and he yanked her down over him.

It was a different kind of desperation from the self-absorbed frenzy with which he had snatched at her before. The smell and touch and outline of his body were all new, as if nothing if them had ever intimated an earlier desire. Now he did not look away, but held her there over him, forcing her hands down so that they pinioned him and he could not, without an effort, have broken free. For the first time she saw terror in his eyes, but as soon as she tried to smooth it away, he wrenched her wrist back again to keep him imprisoned under her. She thought: 'He wants me to murder him.' In that instant she knew that he had been afraid he would not find her there when he came back. She could have told him the idea was nonsense. There was no dimension of hers he did not now inhabit.

For a while afterwards they lay still, wondering what there was to do next. Then 'There's the lawnmower,' Dolly said, 'I wish I could send down and tell them to stop it.'

'Why don't you, if it's annoying?'

'They'll run out of lawns to mow sooner or later.'

They had another silence. A breeze stirred the curtain and blew the smell of the cut grass into the room.

'You'll find my emerald necklace in the boudoir. I haven't worn it for ages, but it just struck me it might suit you.'

'Better than garnets?'

'Oh, twenty times better than garnets.'

They both sniggered like children. Antoine hoisted himself off the bed and ambled into the boudoir.

'Why do you have to shut the door?' she called to him.

'Because that's what one does. There's no point in a door otherwise,' came his voice from within.

In this moment of absolute certainty she recalled Victorine's letter, which, on getting into the room, she had simply flung aside in favour of Antoine. There was something inappropriate in the grace of the maid's handwriting that had always irked her. In tersely elegant phrases, Victorine announced that her mother was not dying after all, that her condition had decidedly improved, and that, assuming it was convenient with Madame, she would make the journey from Nantes tomorrow, hoping to arrive at Aix the following afternoon, thanking Madame for her kindness etcetera etcetera.

For the briefest of moments, the girl's image flashed upon her, a vision of consummate reticence and studied anonymity. She remembered friends saying how lucky she had been to get hold of her. She looked again at the letter, at the little hook on the left diagonal stroke of the *v*, at the neatly turned loop of te *r*, at the *g*'s ornate volute descending from the line, and suddenly apprehended an extraordinary menace in them all. Still naked, Antoine came out of the boudoir, the emeralds lurid against his pale skin. Seeing him, Dolly started to shake with sobs, as his astonished embrace came round her and she heard the clank of the lawnmower.

'Oh, Toto!' she cried.

The Cherry Thief

He made her unhappy. We never expected anything else. By the time she married Lauro, there wasn't a single member of the family who wouldn't have recommended giving him up. None of them could say anything, of course. In those days – and this happened a considerably long time ago – women, as a rule, didn't think of marriage as they do now, like an article you take back to the shop because it's the wrong colour or turns out not to fit. Catch Carlotta doing that sort of thing anyway.

Within six years he was killed, or rather, as the saying somewhat unfairly went, he got himself killed, on the Isonzo when his regiment was holding a bridgehead opposite Gorizia. 'Lauro trod on a mine,' Carlotta said afterwards, as though it had been a silly thing to do. I heard her say it to several people, and it always sounded as if she felt sorry for the mine.

She had, you see, to feel sorry for something. Only when the war was over, and everyone was going through the process of hugging themselves for being alive and swearing it shouldn't happen again, did I perceive that. There's something – you know what I mean – an air, a bloom, a kind of dew falling upon a very young widow, which makes her know her own fascination even in the echoing gloom of those corridors down which she seems perpetually condemned to walk. It makes you feel like saying: 'Come on, you're not really sorry, you don't truly miss him, you can't seriously be grieving, you didn't know him that long so how can you?' and their answering smiles are a confession.

With Carlotta it wasn't like that. Probably she was rather glad than otherwise that Lauro was dead. There were no children, and he had left her decently provided for. Turin during those years was gratifyingly full of young women in search of lovers, but Carlotta could have procured instant devotion just by raising her head. Yet to this she preferred solemnity and reserve, a professional sadness, something she was adept in but which, like a dancer, she had to keep exercised so as to find a reason to exist.

'She's an artist, your sister,' I said one day to Giorgi. He knew exactly what I was talking about.

'Consummate!' he laughed, his chins wobbling over his collar like doughnuts. 'With Carlotta it's always been *qui tollis peccata mundi*. The moral effect on the rest of us was a disaster.'

'She always took the blame, like one of those people in primitive tribes whose function is to eat the sins of the community.'

Giorgi stared at me. There were times when, for all my cousin's weltering, heaving, wheezy, radish-fingered plumpness, you could think him the most beautiful creature alive.

'I can tell you exactly when it got serious with Carlotta,' he began.

'That year they shut the school,' I cut in, 'because of the epidemic, and your father took us all off to Orta early. May, June, I forget when. The year before she married Lauro. When we found the mouth and the birdcages.'

Giorgi's smile was like an embrace. 'Those damned cherries!'

You'd much rather hear about the stone head we found on the table in the empty house and its open mouth which felt warm whenever we put a finger inside it, or the room in that same house stacked to the ceiling with birdcages, or what

48

made us afraid there so that we never went back. Orta was full of such things, or maybe it seemed so to us, since we were of an age that begins to attribute pattern and outline to experience.

Giorgi did this more than I, but he looked to me to put it into words. Why we called him Giorgi nobody knew. His real name was Alberto but it was never used. My aunt, who had a way of inventing causes to match effects, said it was because he was so fat. We accepted this at once, without asking her to explain the process by which the conclusion had been arrived at. It was well known in the family that she treated statements of fact like food set in front of fractious children: once offered, there was no question of them being taken away. So Giorgi he became, to the exclusion of all other sobriquets, fat Giorgi, my cousin, panting and moaning inside his glistening white furls of flesh, one of those blessedly enormous figures who inhabit their obesity with good-humoured grace. That was why I thought him beautiful, though I didn't know it at the time.

Resourceful and calculating in a way which never wholly eroded his innocence, he began each morning at Orta with 'Why don't we?' Why don't we row out to the island, why don't we light all the candles in the church at once, why don't we hide in the hedge by the Swiss doctor's house and make noises at his two daughters as they get on their bicycles, or why don't we make a raid on the Stella d'Italia?

This was our best game, better far than the one which had kept us happy the summer before, when the house had been turned into a castle to be yielded only with the successful conquest of all four floors. Giorgi and I, as sole players, each assumed the various roles with ease, skirmishing across landing and staircase as the beleagured garrison, the messenger on the lathered horse, the governor's daughter in love with the enemy lieutenant, and the patriot who died with 'Italy' on his lips.

We began it again as soon as we arrived, but the game

quickly palled when Giorgi suggested the Stella d'Italia. There, after all, lay real danger; we could be seen from the house, which commanded an ideal prospect of the square, and my aunt, not otherwise very particular about the nature of our associates, was morbidly suspicious of us having anything to do with what she called, in a phrase full of mysterious anthropological vagueness, 'hotel people'. The fact that the Stella d'Italia was the best hotel on the lake, patronised by those to whom at other times, being something of a snob, she gladly deferred, was beside the point. Unless they were business associates of my uncle's or, as occasionally happened, members of the family fetching up there without warning, 'hotel people' were damned in perpetuity. Thus the Stella d'Italia, in reality rather dull and sedate as such places usually are, took on the allure of a necromancer's palace, and its guests, easily identifiable to my aunt's practised eye by their air of seasoned modishness, became interesting entirely because of her invidious distinction. Giorgi and I wanted to know these people. More significantly, we wanted to be them. Much of what has happened since to either of us, I can't help feeling, is linked to this childish fascination.

Like Avernus, it was easier to get into the hotel than out of it. Obsequiousness to new arrivals meant that the attention of porters, pageboys and clerks was seldom likely to be distracted by a child or two slipping cross the hall, and since we were always well dressed there was no obvious incongruity. We simply had to wait for a motor or one of the station carriages to sweep up, before walking briskly in after the porter carrying the last bags to the lift.

We only ever rode in that lift once all summer, I remember, because even Giorgi was frightened by the lift-keeper, an old man of unconscionable grandeur with a wooden leg and, as it seemed, all the medals it had ever been possible to win at Magenta and Solferino draped across his coat like bunting. Otherwise we moved about the place with the insouciant freedom of outlaws, peering through the bedroom doors which chambermaids had left open, dogging the footsteps of those coming and going along the corridors, pretending to wait for some dilatory and invisible parent while we listened to the sad little trio which played every afternoon in the *salon de thé*, or watching the groups of guests coming in from their boating and tennis to be enveloped by the sublime intimacy of those hours immediately before dinner, a time my imagination hallowed with indestructible romance.

Giorgi thought like this as well. Walking in the hotel garden, which the late afternoon made silent as a cloister, and looking up at the windows, we both grew speculative and solemn. By gazing intently at those points where the shutters had not been fully drawn to, or where the breeze – there's always a breeze on the lake – blew the curtains aside, it was possible to glimpse a shape, a movement in the gloom beyond, and to connect its suggestive indistinctiveness with those half-realised evidences of life we had caught earlier in prying after the maids. Those great wardrobe trunks and hatboxes and label-blotched suitcases, those dresses and shoes scattered across the carpet, the cream-pots, hairbrushes, unstoppered scent flasks, single gloves, odd slippers and crumpled handkerchiefs, the letters and diaries at which there was never quite time for us to snatch a glance, the mirrors still stamped, as it were, with their most recent images, and the eloquence of towsled sheets and dented pillows, these things were as significant to us as those papyrus fragments of the lost dramas of the ancients which some Egyptian rubbish heap discloses. Talking familiarly of number 12, number 7 and number 4, we renewed their lives according to the models we had devised for them, refusing to be altogether is heartened when we chanced upon the inevitable banality of the real thing.

There had to be an end to it. We grew over-bold, flaunting our presence before waiters and pages and marching up and down our territory with the arrogance of usurpers. One afternoon, as we dawdled on the steps in front of the hotel, wondering whether to go straight home or stroll down to the jetty and watch the arrivals off the steamer and eat the cake I had providently purloined from one of the tea-tables, Giorgi, twitching my arm, whispered: 'Carlotta!'

'Where?'

'Coming out of the post office. And she's seen us.'

'What about the cake?'

'Put it in your pocket, quick!'

'But it's got jam in it.'

'Never mind, she mustn't see, hurry!'

Into the pocket of my smart English knickerbockers went the offending cake. I felt it crumble between my nervous fingers and its layer of toasted almonds peel off, as Carlotta strode angrily towards us, brandishing her parasol like the falchion of some female warrior out of Tasso.

'Giorgi, Enrico, come here this instant!'

We mooched sullenly to the foot of the steps. It used always to make me cross that there was never any point in lying to her, as if this were some silly game she were too grand to play. We owned up, of course, or rather Giorgi told her as much as he felt she absolutely needed to know, and she shook her head in a way I'd learned obscurely to connect with the alien world of adulthood. Then, giving a little secret smile, she said: 'Now you will both go home and we'll say nothing more about this. And Enrico, you'd better wash your hands, one of them is quite covered in jam.'

'Where are you going?' Giorgi asked.

'Lauro comes to us on Monday and naturally he will stay at the Stella d'Italia, so I am going to see that everything's in order for when he arrives.' For a moment her face had an almost ludicrous brightness within it. 'He is going on a voyage to India.'

'Can we come with you?'

'I'm not going with him, alas. That wouldn't be correct.'

'No, to the hotel,' I said.

'Certainly not. Goodness knows what you've got up to in there already. Now run along, both of you.'

Glancing back wistfully as Carlotta swept through the hall doors, we sloped off across the square. It was as if she had polluted the sanctuary.

'Now I suppose we shan't be able to get inside the hotel for ages,' said Giorgi glumly, 'with Lauro coming. Drat him!'

'Is he nice?'

'Carlotta likes him.'

'Yes, but do you?'

Evading my question, Giorgi exclaimed: 'Hey, there go the Swiss!' as the two girls sailed past on their bicycles.

'I wonder where they go together.'

Giorgi sniggered. 'Perhaps it's that house – that one at the top of the town. I heard Mamma tell Carlotta it was full of bad women. The big gate's got a little one inside it, like a convent.'

'Maybe it is a convent, and your mother's got it wrong. Anyway, why would the Swiss go up there? Come on, let's go home and play L'Attaque before dinner.'

When we reached my uncle's house we found Tilde scrubbing the hall floor. She looked up mournfully as we picked our way across the dry patches. Children are too selfish to be acquainted with pity, but I always felt sorry for Tilde. My aunt was forever scolding and threatening to dismiss her, though she never did, and the other servants seldom spoke to her, because, as I then supposed, she didn't live in the house but came and went each day, invariably with the morsel or two of sewing work for which they paid her extra. Her sagging, bony face moved me the more when I realised the family cared nothing for her. When the cook had a birthday or the gardener brought us his new baby daughter to see, there were smiles and condescension, but Tilde might have been a chair or a table for all the notice that was ever taken of her. At length it became obvious to me that there must be a reason for such consistent shunning, but for the time being I didn't ask why, since I knew I should only receive an evasive answer, even from Giorgi.

The way I found out was quite simple. Giorgi's parents, being of that provident sort who leave nothing to chance, had decreed that his enforced absence from school should not be regarded as merely another holiday. An hour each morning and evening was set aside for assignments furnished by his various teachers, and he wrestled accordingly with isosceles triangles and the mysteries of Foscolo and Manzoni. I, on the other hand, was free do to as I pleased. Since my mother and father were ranked by the rest of the family as feckless ne'er-do-wells who somehow managed to possess money without deserving it, the disposition was at least consistent. When Giorgi protested that it was unfair, my uncle, seeing where the real advantage ought to lie, told him he was a fool and didn't know his own interest.

I was not, as it happened, wasting my time. Orta, the house and its inhabitants, however well I already knew them, were far too absorbing for that. One morning, when Giorgi was engaged on some verses about the expedition of the Thousand to Sicily (having decided, in his fanciful way, that poetry offered the only dignified means of addressing the subject), I slipped out by the garden door, ducked along the path behind the azaleas and was through the gate and on the road down to the town before anyone had time to miss me. Under the grey sky the lake looked curdled and soupy. I moved instinctively, though without any overmastering interest, in the direction of the Stella d'Italia.

When I got to the foot of the steps and saw the spotty-faced, gimlet-eyed pageboy staring at me from the doorway I knew I wasn't brave enough to walk in without Giorgi, who would have answered his challenge with some morsel of wondrous impertinence. Standing at a loss with my hands in my pockets, I caught sight of Tilde. She was coming out of the draper's on the corner of the square, a green parcel clutched under one arm. I knew that when not employed in dusting and sewing for us she earned money by trimming hats, for I had once heard my aunt, with the merest tinge of contempt in her voice, tell Carlotta that Tilde had offered to put a new ribbon on her straw boater when the original had worked loose.

'She had the nerve to tell me it would cost nothing. Of course I said no.'

'Yes, I suppose you would have done,' rejoined Carlotta with that enigmatic coolness which in anyone else would have been taken for insolence. Evidently my aunt did not realise that she was being judged and found wanting, but it was clear to me.

Watching as the gaunt, dingy figure began to climb the hill, I made up my mind to follow her. It was only a boy's game of dogging and tracking at first. Though I guessed she wouldn't look back, I still crouched in gateways and peeped from behind trees, to give the whole thing an air of intrigue. Gradually, however, her stolid, unvarying progress started leading me further away from the part of the town I knew; if I was to find my way home at all easily, the pursuit must soon be abandoned. Heedless curiosity, of the kind which drew me into the corridors and bedrooms of the Stella d'Italia, now drove me to follow Tilde to her very door.

The streets grew narrower and more tortuous. From the open doorways of shops and houses came that thick, dank smell of a world without quite enough room to keep itself clean. Purity was in the air above me, where an infinity of washing, tablecloths like banners, gala festoons of napkins and pillowcases, pairs of drawers ballooning in the breeze, camisoles and blouses bobbing headless from imprisoning clothes-pegs, swayed from the lines strung from balcony to balcony. This, I conceived, was the land of laundries, whence our shirts came back in their full panoply of starched pleats.

Looking up, wondering whether I might see a pair of my stockings or a nightgown hovering there, I wandered out into a ragged little square formed by the openings of three streets around a grove of scrubby plane trees. Tilde all this while hadn't once turned round. She seemed to tiptoe rather than walk across the square, while I sauntered proprietorially after her, as if she were a dog I might whistle up if I chose. In front of the big green gate filling the bulky archway on the furthest corner she stopped, reached up and gave the bell-pull a discreet twitch. The wicket was opened a crack and she was let in, like something the gate had swallowed. For a while I stood motionless, staring at the high grey wall and the arch with its curling volutes, unable to believe that Tilde, the drab, the forlorn, could live anywhere so august.

My incredulity was heightened when one of the carriages from the station, whisking neatly round the edge of the square, drew up before the gate. The two women who got out had the kind of self-assured smartness I associated with people whose bedrooms I pried into at the hotel. They appeared to have been sharing a joke with the driver, and the three of them remained for a while laughing retrospectively in that way which always sounds as though whatever was originally funny is having the air let out of it. One of them tugged at the bell-pull imperiously while the other gave a rap on the door with her umbrella handle, after which both of them exploded into laughter again. Then the wicket opened once more, much wider than before, and the cab-driver handed their bags in and took his fare.

In turning the carriage he caught sight of me, gaping still at the arch. He reined up sharply and cried: 'Hey, little boy, what are you standing there for? This isn't a place for youngsters like you! Clear off!'

He took up his whip as if he'd use it on me and I ran off among the trees. As he clattered away, I heard him call out jocularly: 'When you're older!'

People telling stories of this kind invariably pretend to a knowledge beyond their years and I suppose I ought to claim that I understood exactly what the coachman meant, but that wouldn't be true. By the time I reached home I was pondering whether or not to ask Giorgi. He, I was certain, would have the answer.

An immense, burnished motor car stood in the drive. Lauro, of course, I'd forgotten. When I walked into the drawing room I felt a spurt of peevish annoyance at him for arriving like this. It meant that my expedition was not to be enquired into, so I hated him at once. I hated the way he exhibited his teeth when he laughed, his bulbous, glittering eyes, the hairy backs of his hands and the waxed points of his moustache. Above all I hated to see Carlotta standing behind him as he sat, looking down at him with a smiling compassion, as though wanting to know what on earth she could possibly do with such a polished article. Repelled by his gleaming masculinity I gave him a cold handshake and hoped he would dislike me.

They were all looking at photographs he'd brought and tittering good-naturedly as they passed them about. Lauro playing tennis, Lauro in a striking attitude on a horse in the Parco Valentino, Lauro doing a handstand while wearing evening clothes. I wondered whether he ever did anything so ordinary as sitting still.

The maid came in to tell us that luncheon was served. Giorgi stared at me grimly, as if I owed him an explanation, and passed a last photograph over as my aunt and uncle led the way out of the room.

'It's his wrestling club,' he said, and wobbled off into the hall laughing insanely.

For a moment I stood glancing at it, a picture of a dozen elaborately developed young men, Lauro grinning among them, in leotards and boots, hands on hips, chests thrust out, evidently delighted with the figures they cut, seeing, as it were, the photograph before it was taken. It's too late now for me to remember the exact emotion I felt when I looked at this, but something in the sheer offered luxuriance of curves, bulges and hollows made me turn my back to the doorway. Contemplating Lauro thus, hairy and lavish before the camera, I loathed him still more, only now without knowing why.

'Enrico, we're waiting for you!'

It was Carlotta, who snatched the picture from me.

'Too silly, aren't they?' she laughed. 'Mother wouldn't let me see it just now.' Then in a voice not altogether joyful she muttered: 'My naughty boy,' and only when I was at the table did I realise she hadn't meant me.

'So you lied to me?'

'But you knew that.'

'It still shocks me, even after fifteen years or however long it is. I need reminding, so that I can be outraged all over again.' Giorgi ran his fingers ruminatively across the grey slopes of his waistcoat. 'Why?'

'To be revenged on you for knowing everything. I'll never forget your face when you discovered.'

'I didn't have the chance to be angry then. Maybe that's why I've never forgiven you.' His melting gaze held me. 'Get us another cocktail, there's a dear fellow. God, the women here are disgusting, we'd have done better to go to Gambrinus. Who knows, there might have been one for you.'

'For you there's always something, isn't there? It's what comes of looking like Pola Negri mated with an elephant.'

Giorgi kicked me and guffawed. 'They can't resist me. It's because they think I'm going to cry. Women like that, you know.'

'They couldn't resist Lauro, and he probably never cried in his life.'

'That's what he wanted you to think. I bet he roared when he thought the Austrians were going to make a hole in his smart uniform.'

There was a silence between us as we remembered him, not with any pleasure at what he was, but because of what he had made us feel.

'Carlotta guessed,' I said, tracing my initials in the spilt beer on the table. 'About Lauro.'

'After the cherries,' said Giorgi.

'No, before.'

Lauro always cheated when we played L'Attaque. I don't know whether it's played nowadays. Two opposing battle lines, composed of small pieces of card on metal stands, each with a picture of a soldier on it, are drawn up on either side of a river, and the object is to get as many of your men as possible over the bridge and past the mines, risking attack as you go. Since the blank side of each piece is facing you and victory at every challenge is always given to the superior rank – though only the Spy, a louche figure lurking behind a tree in a Homburg hat and fur-collared overcoat, may take the General – the dangers are considerable. The skill consists in trying to remember, as the board is cleared, where you opponent has positioned his best men.

I can't tell you how he managed to cheat, I just know he did. Carlotta knew it too, sitting beside him and applauding whenever he made a successful manoeuvre or sent in a sapper to blow up a mine. She seemed all the while to be teasing him, as though she guessed that his need to prove himself the winner must be satisfied even in so trifling an exercise, and it embarrassed me that Lauro could never grasp the full import of her sarcasms.

The pattern repeated itself a few days later when they took to the tennis court. Lauro had evidently lost no time in making friends while at the Stella d'Italia and was eager to get up a doubles match with himself and Carlotta against a young Milanese banker and his wife.

'And you two', Carlotta announced in her most incontro-vertibly decisive tone, 'will come with us.'

'Good heavens, what on earth do you want with them?' cried my uncle, whose view of children oscillated between a vague benevolence and a thorough contempt for their use-lessness.

'They will come along to see fair play,' she said with a hint of a smile. Lauro, guffawing, cried 'Bravo!' He hadn't understood.

Revisit the Stella d'Italia after the absence created by Lauro's arrival was to make me realise how much, in that short period, I had outgrown it. I responded to Giorgi's specu-lations as to what might have altered in the interim with dishonest politeness, and to find that the orchestrina still played in the *salon de thé*, that the ancient hero of Solferino was still operating the lift, and that the pageboys' hair still glistened with pomade was reassuring to my general sense that none of it mattered any longer. From the tennis court I glimpsed the roof of the house with the arch and the trees in the scrubby little square, peering furtively over the shoulder of the town.

'They've closed the shutters in number 27,' muttered Giorgi, nudging me.

'Yes,' I said.

We sat on the grass and watched the couples ducking and lunging on either side of the net. The Milanese had that spruce finish calculated to appeal, for different reasons, to both Lauro and Carlotta. It was obvious, too, that though they were much better players, they had the grace to defer to their opponents whenever the chance arose for the latter to score a point. When Giorgi accused me of watching the game too closely and not paying attention to something funny he'd just said, I found it impossible to explain that it wasn't the game I was watching but the participants, Lauro flinging himself histriorically at the net, Carlotta involved far more seriously in ironic comment on his performance than on her volleys and serve, and the two Milanese darting across the grass with a relaxed efficiency intended to keep the game going in just the right measure of enthusiasm. They permitted Lauro, what was more, to make his own liberal interpretation of the rules, quite as if Carlotta had issued prior instructions to that effect. Cross as I still was with her, I found I was starting to enjoy the spectacle of Lauro making an ass of himself, and felt almost sorry when the pair decided they'd had enough and the two young women bunched together confidentially for a walk across the garden, leaving Lauro and his friend to sit down with a meditative cigarette on one of the benches under the cypress hedge. Giorgi got up, dusting the grass off his voluminous bottom.

'Let's go up to the second floor landing,' he said, 'they must be cleaning it still.'

'No; I don't want to.'

'Oh, come on, Carlotta won't know.'

'I don't care about Carlotta, I'm not coming, that's all.'

He looked at me mistrustfully. 'You're not frightened, are you?'

'No, I just don't want to go into the hotel.'

Irritated, he turned and walked off up the steps, with that surprising dignity of bearing which was his to command when he needed it. I knew we shouldn't quarrel – we never did that – but I was keener than ever that he shouldn't know where I had been on the morning of Lauro's arrival.

In fact I had been there on two occasions since, both of them during Giorgi's lesson times. I never spent more than five minutes or so in the square, standing well back under the trees, so as to avoid many repetition of my encounter with the impertinent cab-driver, and hoping that I might see Tilde, like some dusty insect in her crumpled black skirt and battered bonnet, being subsumed as before into the silent house with the arch and the blank windows. The place vouchsafed nothing, however, beyond its intractable emptiness, enough in the end to frighten me away down the hill and back into the safety of my uncle's garden.

Looking up again towards that sly-looking roof, I felt the weight of an insufferable boredom which I'd rather have died than alleviate by running into the hotel to join Giorgi. A sudden pang of homesickness for our pokey, unlovely flat in Turin, with my sisters banging on the piano and the maid putting my father's medicines beside his place at table with a reverent attention to the symmetrical arrangement of phials and pillboxes, was soon followed by a resentment at Lauro for having barged into the cosily ordered sameness of our lives here at Orta with such proprietorial selfishness.

This must have been why, when I caught sight of Carlotta unexpectedly alone at the lake's edge, I was overcome with a wish to protect her. She stood at the top of the steps, shading her eyes to stare out across the sunlit water to the island. The breeze twitched the edges of her tennis dress, but otherwise she remained as motionless as I was in my sudden absorption, gazing at the island as if it were about to yield some long-awaited answer.

I wasn't in love with her. Adults are fond of naming children's emotions, like the masters of slaves who gave them names so as to establish ownership, but the true identity of such feelings, childhood once left, is as mysterious to us as some language palaeology still labours to decipher. So we called it love, Giorgi and I, when discussing it that evening at the café, because there was nothing else that would answer, though it felt more as if I had brought her up and was anxious lest the effects of my education should be spoiled. Cross, nervous, scornful Carlotta, who, if she thought me at all, considered me a prying, ill-mannered scrap of a boy, as bare of knowledge as I was clothed in presumption.

'She didn't move. She stayed like that until her friend came back, and that was when I ran up the path and hid behind the hedge and heard Lauro telling the Milanese about his conquests in Turin. Did I mention that?'

Giorgi rubbed his eyes and yawned. 'Probably not. Added it to your other suppressions, I expect.'

'There was the bit about him crossing the road. I must have told you. It was in Corso San Muarizio. There was this

girl he'd just thrown over, she met him as he was coming out
of a shop. He'd been buying a tie – I remember that bit –
can't you just imagine Lauro buying a tie? She chased him
up the street, he said. Fearfully embarrassing, as he passed
several people he knew and had to pretend he was in a hurry
and couldn't stop to talk.'

'What about his car?'

'Hadn't got it just then. Lots of traffic that day anyway.
They got up as far as Via Montebello and Lauro heard the
girl shouting after him. You must recall this, surely?'

'I don't know why I should. Go on.'

'Apparently she kept shouting "Lauro, how can you treat
me like this? Lauro, what have I done?" – you know the kind
of thing women say to make you feel guilty. When he decided
to make a dash for it, he saw three trams coming one way
and two the other, but he just plunged out into the road and
somehow got between them. When he was in the middle he
heard her coming after him, screaming "Lauro, how can you
treat me like this?" at the top of her voice, and he couldn't
believe it when the tram jammed on its brakes and there she
was lying in the roadway. But not hurt or anything.'

'Oh yes, I remember now,' cried Giorgi, cackling with
laughter, 'he was so cross that he slapped her face in front of
the passers-by, and then hailed a cab and drove off. Wasn't
that it? I rather admire his effrontery. Though I must say I
wonder what I'd do now if I knew that the man who was
engaged to my sister had been fornicating with shopgirls at
the same time.'

'Perhaps that's why you forgot.'

I did not, as it happens, communicate this to Giorgi until
several years afterwards. Lurking behind the hedge, I felt
more curiosity than outrage: it was, after all, quite what I'd
have expected Lauro to do. Yet I was even more determined
to shield Carlotta from him, if only I knew how. Across the
dinner table I fixed him with a morose gaze, as if that, com-

bined with everything he had unknowingly permitted me to hear, would wither him up. He lost to my uncle at chess and I was bitterly exultant, nursing a gloomy joy in the corner of the drawing room, where I sat pretending to read Jules Verne.

It was the first memorably warm evening of the year, when the dusk seemed genuinely reluctant to turn into night and a languid passivity, numbing spontaneous impulse, covered us all like dustsheets on pieces of furniture. Now and then some insect, a moth or a cockchafer, flew in and batted against the lamps, but my aunt and Carlotta never raised their heads from sewing. Occasionally Giorgi, doing maths exercises which involved much scratching and chewing of the pen, would glance furtively at me with a look which meant that under no circumstances should either of us do anything to draw the grown-ups' attention to the fact that it was long past our bedtime. My uncle, with a pair of very small scissors, was snipping sections out of the newspaper, a habit I had never known him to relax and whose object was always a mystery to me. Only Lauro seemed restless, sitting there pressing his hands together and periodically making that tea-tasting noise for which there ought to be a special name as a universal expression of discontent. The lamplight glistened on the oiled sleekness of his hair and the pomaded ends of his moustache, giving him an air of slightly vulgar uselessness, like those presents given us by grateful servants which we are too embarrassed either to place on view or to throw away. If it hadn't been for my devotion to Carlotta, I'd have felt sorry for Lauro. After all, I thought, I know what he is.

Just as the final illusion of daylight spent itself, a cuckoo started calling in the woods below the house. It was such an unlikely occurrence that everyone started up as if this had been an omen, and my aunt, vexed at the sheer impertinence, made a little clucking noise of vexation.

'Really, at this hour!'

My uncle laughed. 'Do you expect cuckoos to keep regular hours?'

'Whoever heard of one singing in the dark? What nonsense!'

'Perhaps', said Lauro, 'it isn't a real cuckoo. Perhaps somebody presses a button and sets it off by electricity, eh?'

Nobody bothered to laugh at this, so he did it for himself, then turned to Carlotta as though for approval. I wondered if he were afraid of her, she looked at him so seriously.

'Enrico, stop staring at people like that!' she cried, with a vehemence that caught me quite off guard. 'It's high time you and Giorgi went to bed. You've got into some bad habits, the pair of you. Giorgi, take those books upstairs, and Enrico, don't forget to leave your boots out for Annunziata to polish in the morning. They're a disgrace, goodness knows where you go to get them so dirty.'

Giorgi hoisted himself grumpily to his feet, and the bossy girl stood over us as we said our goodnights. Because we knew it annoyed her, we went through our customary parade of mock-exhaustion, dragging ourselves slowly from banister to banister, gasping and slithering as we mounted the stairs, and falling over one another in a heap when we reached the top. Washing to perfunctorily, we were made to go through the process again, as a prelude to the dreadful business of having our hair brushed, an action Carlotta carried out with the intensity of gardener raking flowerbeds. Then we got into bed, smarting from the indignity, and she stood there for a moment, her face suffused with a sudden indulgence.

'My boots,' I murmured as she made to switch off the light, 'I forgot to put them downstairs for Annunziata.'

'On with your slippers and take them down yourself. I've things to do for Mamma.'

'Can't you do it? My hair might get untidy and then you'd have to brush it again.'

'Don't make excuses, Enrico, that's the first sign of dishonesty.'

So I scrambled out of bed and went down with the offending boots into the hall. There was something friendly in its gloom that made me want to linger. I put the boots by the table near the front door where we always left them, and stayed there in the shadow listening. From the drawing room came the sound of Lauro's braying laughter, no doubt inspired by something he himself had said. Upstairs I could hear Carlotta moving swiftly to and fro, opening and shutting the cupboards. There was slight rustling sound from the hem of her skirt as it brushed the carpet. Outside in the darkness the cuckoo persisted, lonely and monotonous.

Suddenly her face appeared over the bannisters. 'Enrico!'

But I hung back in the warm darkness, full of an inarticulate sorrow for her. If I stayed there long enough, maybe at last I should get her to weep.

'Enrico, where are you? Come up this instant and get into bed!'

Swish swish went the hem of her dress as the cuckoo kept on in the hollow of the wood.

There was no point in telling me not to stare. I watched her at every opportunity, fascinated, in a way unaccountable to me now, by her defencelessness. I felt it was what she wanted me to know, under her pose of martinet and cynic, by which, as she must have guessed, I wasn't perplexed any longer. Lauro existed, I since believe, all the gloss and plenitude and vigour of him, simply to accomplish her expectations. Now and then I've had this waking dream of them, the beautiful pair, locked together on their wedding night. The muscles of his black glisten with sweat as he strains to an orgasm, accompanied by his operatic gasps and moans. She, in the dream's authentic implausibility, remains totally silent: it is not indeed clear that she is actually breathing. Her face, always plainly visible, is transfigured by a broad grin of irresistible amusement which turns, as Lauro comes, into a peal of laughter. I suppose it might actually have been like that, but Lauro wouldn't seriously have known how to deal with anything so unexpected as his bride giggling uncontrollably at his nuptial virtuosity. Yet in a sense it had happened many times already.

Somebody else understood that besides me. One morning they were getting ready to go out for a ride in the motor and Tilde was mopping the tiles in the hall because the cat had puked on them. He was one of those venerable, filmy-eyed grandees whom the servants overfeed either to ingratiate themselves with their employers or else in the hope that some feline apoplexy will relieve them of a boring responsibility. Giorgi and I used to enjoy watching him throw up, in that contemplative fashion cats adopt, but it invariably fell to Tilde to clear away his messes. As she did so we would both crouch on all fours and imitate his little shakes and wheezes, falling about with delight at the perfection of our mimicry.

That morning, though we hadn't caught the cat *in flagrante delicto*, we were still determined to go through the performance, and it was thus, rocking with laughter as Tilde discreetly ran her mop to and fro across the floor, that Carlotta and Lauro found us when they came downstairs.

'Get up, get up, what on earth are you doing?' cried Carlotta.

Giorgi, for whom it was of course more difficult to do as he was bidden, answered sweetly: 'We're being Fufo being sick.'

'Yes, he goes like this,' I added, 'euhp, euhp, and then he looks at it and walks away.'

Giorgi went off into paroxysms as I made the noise, and Lauro, to whom this was calculated to appeal, was tickled pink.

Carlotta, resolutely unimpressed, merely said: 'Anyway, you look utterly ridiculous in that posture, Giorgi. Doesn't he look ridiculous, Lauro?'

To her surprise, rather to mine also, Lauro answered: 'No, actually I think he looks quite sweet.'

Giorgi, visibly not pleased at that, drew himself upright and said stiffly: 'Well, *we* thought it was funny.'

Carlotta shrugged. 'At your age . . .' I knew she included Lauro in the dismissal.

It was just then that I caught Tilde looking at her. If I had to describe that look now, I should reach for phrases such as 'interested compassion' or 'pained concern', but maybe it wasn't anything of the sort. What I never forgot was the sense conveyed by the almost presumptuous calm in her glance that she and I shared the same apprehensions about Carlotta. Accordingly I never took my eyes off her until she had picked up her mop and bucket, curtseyed and flitted off like a shabby black moth towards the kitchen, but the little hint of sympathy between us vanished almost as soon as it had appeared, and I never saw it again.

'The cherries come after that bit.'

'Not exactly.' I was being deliberately obstructive.

'Well, damn it all, what else?' cried Giorgi crossly. An old man at the next table gazed at us with unconcealed disapproval. 'There wasn't anything else, was there?'

'Yes.'

'Don't get laconic with me. You're just doing it for the effect. Because that was when you started having secrets.'

'Precisely. So why do I have to tell you everything now?'

Giorgi put his head on one side. 'Because you've always loved me,' he said shamelessly. But it wouldn't do, I was inexorable.

'There really was something else. You may not remember, but I think it matters.'

'Oh, well, what?'

'Lauro went back to Turin without any lunch. Apparently they stopped at the Stella d'Italia on their way back from the drive and he went into the hotel to pick up his post. He told Carlotta there was a telegram. She didn't believe him, of course.'

'Nobody ever believes there's a telegram. Carlotta's was the religion of scepticism besides. Anyway he went, didn't he? To fuck with one of his shopgirls, I suppose.' Giorgi supped his beer reflectively. 'Actually, Rico, there was a time when I thought he might have been in love with her. Carlotta, I mean. But she'd never have allowed it. He had to be her naughty boy, so she couldn't believe in the telegram. On principle she just couldn't. Tell me what happened next, there's a dear chap.'

Neither of us ever forgot the triumph in her face as she swept down the garden towards us. My uncle and aunt looked at their daughter with evident complacency, as if taking all the credit for her, but to me there was something unattractive in the deviousness of her smile. With a boy's illogical absoluteness I felt I had a right to know what emotions she had just tidied away so skilfully. In my way I was a sceptic too: I didn't for one moment believe that her happiness was entirely contained in the basket she carried on one arm.

'Look!' she cried, 'aren't they beautiful? The first of the season. A dear old man was selling them by the roadside, so Lauro insisted on buying some, and now he won't be able to eat them.'

'Cherries!' exclaimed Giorgi, 'that means we needn't have Geltrude's boring apple cake tonight. Or tomorrow night for that matter. Or ever. We can live off cherries for the rest of the summer.'

'Can we really have them at dinner?' I asked doubtfully.

'I can't think they'll improve with keeping,' said Carlotta, 'though it does seem a shame to eat them.'

They were as beautiful as she declared. The pinkish-red *marasche*, with that sensuous amplitude in their ripe curves and the promise of a certain surprising bitterness in the after-taste which no other cherry seems to possess, they lay tumbled into a glistening heap against the sides of the basket. For an instant we said nothing, transfigured from our natural prose by the sheer lavishness of the offered vision.

'We shall have to eat them for dinner,' said my uncle

gloomily, 'otherwise we'll grow too fond of them and want them to last for ever.'

'Don't poke at them, Giorgi, there's a dear,' my aunt said.

'I wanted to see if Carlotta was fooling us,' he rejoined, as though knowing from the outset that the notion was absurd. I felt I could have told him otherwise. In themselves the cherries were a kind of lie.

'Well, they're not made of wax but you can't eat any of them now,' she said, suddenly whisking the basket away, and bearing it before us like a trophy as we followed her into the house.

At lunch, I remember, the talk, for some reason, was all about Tilde. My aunt, perpetually threatening to send her away on the obscure pretext that her presence brought disrepute to the family, had now decided to act in earnest and announced that she would give the woman notice tomorrow. Carlotta seemed rather in favour of it being that afternoon, but her mother needed time to prepare herself.

'I'm so bad at it, it's not in my nature,' sighed my aunt, pressing her hand to her forehead in a little pantomime of distress. 'Thank goodness one doesn't have to do it every day.'

'I really can't think why you have to do it at all,' my uncle said. 'To hear the pair of you talk, one would think the poor creature had committed a crime.'

'It isn't that, only I don't like having her in the house. It's bad for the other servants. Especially with a daughter like that.'

'I can't look at her,' said Carlotta sombrely; 'it makes me . . . it frightens me.'

From the other end of the table, across the familiar landscape of the white cloth with its dishes and bottles, my uncle stared at the two women as if he hardly knew them. The genial serenity in his countenance was suddenly replaced with scorn.

'I should have thought "a daughter like that" could make

enough money to keep them both without too much trouble,' he muttered with a little dry chuckle and turned to his plate again.

My aunt spluttered somewhat and looked nervously at Carlotta, but neither of them said anything. We continued eating in an unaccustomed silence, broken finally by Giorgi, who rounded on his sister.

'Of course, you're not going to tell us about Tilde's daughter, are you? And you probably pay the servants not to tell us. But we'll find out one day, even if we have to ask Tilde herself. Then you'll see.'

I had never heard him so savage with her. There was another silence, during which my uncle gazed at us with a scientist's clinical scrutiny. Then, without warning, Carlotta got up from her chair, walked swiftly round the table and started to cuff her brother smartly across the sides of his face. Under the rain of blows Lauro sat quite still, his eyes smouldering with anger. When Carlotta had had enough, or deemed, at any rate, that he had had enough, she swept from the room, as if the act had purged her of any association with the rest of us.

After lunch Giorgi went into the garden to sulk, my aunt decided that a headache was appropriate and my uncle, smiling enigmatically, retreated to his study with a newspaper and a pair of scissors. I had left my Jules Verne in the drawing room, but seeing Carlotta there I judged it prudent to hang back a little. She stood quite still, staring at something she held in her hand, a piece of paper as I supposed. Then I heard her laugh softly and murmur: 'Silly boys,' and when she came out into the hall and saw me, she smiled, saying: 'Not you, Rico dear,' before sailing away to her room in abstracted amusement.

I picked up what she had been looking at. It was the photograph of Lauro and his wrestling club he had brought on the first day of his visit. I couldn't for the life of me understand why she thought it so silly. To me there was something obscurely repulsive, as there had been when I first saw it, in the way whereby the sitters appeared to thrust themselves at the camera as if clamorous for notice. The archness of their posing, the sense of a contrived ease in the way they sat or sprawled, and Lauro in their midst, his waxed moustache agleam, seemed more dangerous than absurd. I put it down as though it would stick to my fingers, found my book and went upstairs. Over the banisters I could see the cherries which the maid had placed in a dish on the hall table. In this context of sacramental unreality it was easy to see why the grown-ups were so reluctant to eat them. A curse seemed to lie on anyone who so much as threatened to violate their impacted brightness.

It was a sultry afternoon, with a slight haze over the little patch of lake I could see from my bedroom window. Unwilling to read or sleep, full of a fretful, directionless ennui which the malign photograph seemed to have stirred in me, I wandered over and looked out across the gardens of the neighbouring houses to the clustered rooftops up the hillside. The thin line of yellow coping and the sharply angled pediment which rounded off the prospect were those of the house with the arch. At this moment I could rather have fancied going there. Then I saw Tilde slipping down the side path among the azaleas.

From here her quick, uneven movements looked like those of some furtive little spider. I could see the tatty black shawl flapping over her shoulders and the old patched carpet bag she always carried. Then she stopped to glance back, I drew swiftly away from the window and decided in that instant to run downstairs and follow her. As I made towards the door, I found Giorgi rolling along the landing towards me, the picture of wretchedness, his great inky eyes glistening with tears.

'You've been crying,' I said obtusely, patting him on the shoulder in a way that appeared suitably wise and elderly.

He came in and sat down on his bed, which creaked resignedly in response.

'Beast,' he snuffled, 'she's a beast and I hate her. She only did it because she's cross that Lauro's gone and she hasn't anyone left to tease. I hate her.'

'I thought you hated Lauro.'

'Not as much as I hate her. She doesn't like Lauro anyway, she just wants to marry him so that she can have her own house and be rich and drive in his motor. I think that's horrible.'

It was the first time I had heard Giorgi sit in judgement on his sister thus. Awed by his intensity, I sat watching as he stared fixedly at the carpet, wiping his nose from time to time with the back of his hand. Actually I was also a trifle put out that his arrival in this state should have prevented me from following Tilde. But then, just as I was pondering a means of getting decently out of the house without seeming to care too little for my cousin in his present state, there came the sound of Carlotta's voice, loud and alarmed, in the hall.

Giorgi and I hurried downstairs to find my uncle and aunt and the maid Annunziata emerging, like characters in a play, 'from different doors', to confront Carlotta, the picture of helpless rage.

'They've gone!' she cried. 'Look! Someone's taken them, and they haven't even left the bowl!'

The cherries, which only half an hour earlier had defied the merest touch of a profane hand, had utterly disappeared, leaving the grey marble surface of the table on which they had stood almost vocal in its emptiness. Staggered, as if some malign mythological creature had snatched them from our midst even as we began to contemplate eating them, we turned our accusing eyes on Annunziata, who immediately proclaimed, in that tone of injured virtue servants always assume, that she hadn't any idea what had happened to them and that in any case she'd been downstairs helping Geltrude, who had a bad wrist, to tie the threads round the *polpette*.

She finished with a little sniff, as though to imply that an exercise so trivial as stealing a bowl of cherries was beneath serious consideration.

'It might have been a gipsy,' said my aunt; 'they do walk into houses and steal things, you know. Luisa Borra said that one of them was caught taking spoons off the dining table in that big villa by the bend as you go up to Vacciago. She'd come in, bold as brass, and was putting them in a napkin. They'd laid the table for dinner, though it was . . .' Her voice tailed off when she realised none of us thought her theory very plausible.

'Could've been the cat,' muttered Giorgi, glowering sullenly at his sister.

My uncle was the most philosophic. 'There,' he said, putting a fatherly arm around Carlotta, 'they've gone, and most likely we'll never get them back. We shall have to put locks on the gates and go in and out with a key. A bore, but there it is.' he laughed with his usual good-humoured cynicism, and said to Annunziata: 'I don't suppose Geltrude could be persuaded to knock us up one of her cakes, could she?'

Silently Carlotta opened the front door and stood on the steps, obscurely pensive. We boys, for no particular reason, followed her. It seemed odd to me that nobody had mentioned Tilde, and I now perceived what a singular opportunity lay in my way. Turning round to make sure that my aunt and uncle were not still in the hall, I announced, with dramatic insouciance, that I knew where the cherries were.

'You!' cried Giorgi peevishly.

'Oh, what nonsense!' exclaimed Carlotta. 'Enrico, you can't possibly know unless you're hiding them. Whyever didn't I think of that? It's the sort of silly thing you'd do. Are you hiding them?'

'No, of course not, I've better things to do than hide cherries from you,' I said, emphasising the last word with Olympian disdain. 'Do you seriously want to know where they are?'

'How on earth did you find out?' said Giorgi.

'I'm not going to tell you that. But I'll tell you where they are.' I paused, luxuriating in my power. 'Or maybe I'll show you instead.'

'You will tell me immediately,' said Carlotta, but the tremor in her voice gave her away and I had to stop myself from exultant laughter.

'I'll show you on one condition,' I announced.

She was about to remonstrate again, but realising it was useless she flung her hands resignedly together, crying: 'Oh . . . oh, very well, what?'

'That you'll promise not to tell Uncle and Aunt. Just go and fetch your hat and say you're taking us for a walk.'

She started obediently into the house. The degree of my new-found authority quite unnerved me. I dared not look at Giorgi.

'You lying little squirt!' he hissed. 'You lied to me.'

'No I didn't. I never said anything about the cherries to you.'

'Why not?' He was on the edge of blubbering once more. 'I would have told you.'

'Bet you wouldn't. Anyway it's my secret and now you're going to find out, so I'm not lying, am I?'

He kicked the step and growled: 'Liar! You're as bad as she is,' as Carlotta, her hat jammed rather than pinned on to her head, emerged from the house, looking guilty as I'd never seen her before, and we set off at the most unconvincing pace for an afternoon walk.

Actually I had no more idea of where the cherries were than either of my companions. The notion that Tilde had slipped off with them in her bag was simply an intelligent guess calculated to furnish a pretext for satisfying my curiosity about the house with the arch. As we hurried along, I soon realised that only by keeping absolutely silent would I achieve my present ambition. To my cousins' increasingly irritated questioning I was ominously unresponsive, as the streets got steeper and poor Giorgi began to lag behind Carlotta like ballast thrown off a tall ship. I could see her growing ever more doubtful as the lane narrowed and the washing lines began. It did not occur to me then that our escapade was leading her into a territory as threatening as it was alien, and I couldn't understand why she seemed to find everything so distasteful when the object was simply to recover her lost *marasche*.

When finally we came out into the little square with the scrubby trees, she exclaimed: 'Thank goodness! Here at least one can breathe a little.'

And we did, I saying nothing, she biting her finger nervously, as we stared down at the Stella d'Italia and the island and the lake, from which the haze had lifted somewhat so that we could see the dim contours of the hills, while Giorgi puffed and flailed towards us under the napkins and pillowcases.

'And now?' said Carlotta.

I looked balefully up at her. Perhaps I did catch something of what was really happening and wanted to find out whether she understood as well. Like some phantom of legend, whose dumbness is the condition of its obedience, I led the way across the square towards the house with the arch without once turning round or answering. Then I glowered at her again, as if the poor girl were somehow to know that it was her duty to pull at the bell-handle. Pull nevertheless she did, and we heard its distinctive clank within.

'Once we got inside, what happened? I don't exactly recall.'

Everything which happened after that is still incredible to Giorgi and me. We've never talked about it with Carlotta, though we spent much of that evening in the café pulling it this way and that between us, trying to make it acceptable to our adult orthodoxy. It was as if, from the instant of Carlotta ringing the bell, some unseen hand had assumed control, on whose magical dispensation every sort of responsibility might conveniently be laid. Yet as a solution that was useless. The occasion belonged to us three alone, and thus it has remained, defiantly immovable in the memory ever since.

'You behaved as though you owned the place,' Giorgi said. 'I half suspected you had got inside before.'

'It felt just like the Stella d'Italia,' I said, then corrected myself. 'I mean that was just how it didn't feel. It was like coming into the possession of an inheritance. That woman who opened the door to us was one of the two I'd watched getting out of the cab in the square. She had a bit less paint on, but I recognised her at once. And that was why I just boldly went in and asked her where Tilde was.'

Giorgi exploded with laughter. 'Carlotta almost died when you said that. Because she'd guessed where we were. She wasn't supposed to know, but my mother had let fall things about Tilde doing the ironing for those bad girls and having a daughter who wasn't quite the thing in the virtue department. The woman must have thought we were crazy. But why didn't she ask us to leave, or at least to say who we were?'

I stared hard at the pink tabletop, flecked with white like a slice of mortadella. 'I don't know,' I said, 'I don't know why she didn't.'

'But why not?' repeated Giorgi. 'Jesus Christ, Rico, we saw it, two boys of twelve, we saw the lot, or nearly all. Those women in stays at the top of the stairs. I'd never even seen a pair of stays on a woman before.'

'And those men with cigars in that big room with the looking-glasses watching the two girls dancing in their peignoirs while some old bird was thrashing away at the piano.'

'And those ghastly pictures of fat nymphs with their legs in the air which you stopped me looking at.'

'I didn't stop you looking at them, I just wanted you to hurry up. Do you know what I kept wondering?'

'What?'

'Whether Lauro ever went there. I kept thinking about

him all the time. I thought "Now I know,about him and Carlotta." '

Giorgi gave a great fat sigh. 'Ah, Carlotta. We've rather put off thinking about her, haven't we? She never flinched from it. Never gave the least sign of reluctance or ruffled propriety when the woman asked her to follow. You'd have expected, wouldn't you, that she'd want to whisk us off at once and tell my parents. But there was a sort of passivity about her, a dumb absorption. I noticed it even then. God knows if I can account for it now.'

His words brought her before me, in all the impenetrable single-mindedness of her revolt.

'Her eyes,' I said, 'they were bright with deduction.'

The room into which we were shown, or rather deposited by our guide, whose impatience had made itself clear as she led us through the maze of corridors, was a kind of annexe to the kitchen of the establishment with smells to match. Its single small window seemed to exist for ornament rather than light, and a door suggested further rooms beyond. For furniture there were a couple of very old, battered-looking black chairs, a worn strip of matting and a positively antediluvian chaise-longue, on one end of which, close to a lamp on a table, sat Tilde mending a stocking.

She must have known why we had come. Her surprise was seeing us there at all. Yet from the first there was a curious dignity in the way whereby, putting her work to one side and rising from the sofa, she managed to imply that this wretched domain was in some way hers, on which we were the impudent trespassers. For a moment we stood in sheepish silence. Any pride I might have taken in unmasking a culprit had vanished utterly, and Carlotta, for the first time in her life, was quite inadequate to the situation.

'You'll be wanting them back,' said Tilde with laconic resignation. 'I didn't think . . .' She paused. There was a little catch in her voice. 'I didn't think you'd find out so soon.'

'Did you really take them?' asked Carlotta, less in accusation than from a simple wish to know. Tilde nodded.

'Then I think', said Carlotta in a thin voice whose authority was a desperate illusion, 'that you had better return them to us.'

'Yes, yes, at once.' Tilde was subdued again. I felt something like resentment at it. With her little bird-like movements she tidied her sewing away and then approached the farther door to tap on it apprehensively. Opening it a crack, she peered round and said something we couldn't hear to whoever was in the next room. No answering voice came, and when she turned to us again it was with genuine anxiety.

'Shall I wake her? Do you think I ought to? She couldn't sleep all last night, poor love, so I thought if she went off now for a bit it might do her some good. She was that poorly I didn't know what to do, and you don't like to call out the doctor when it's so late. But do you think I should? Perhaps I'd better.'

She spoke to herself rather than us. We weren't listening properly to her, absorbed as each of us was in a wider reality.

While Tilde, resolving her doubts, went again towards the door, Carlotta, by now quite distraught with embarrassment, mouthed: 'Her daughter,' as if we hadn't gathered that already.

Then Tilde stuck her head out of the room and whispered: 'You can come in, she's awake; she'd like to see you. If you'd be so kind.'

Nervously, animated more by tactful compliance than curiosity, we entered the little bedroom. In its wretched, apologetic fashion it was a more cheerful place than Tilde's sitting room, not shunning the daylight as the rest of the house seemed so determined on doing. The walls were decorated with pages cut from illustrated papers, an oleograph of the Madonna cradling the infant Jesus, and one of those gold-bordered almanack-holders with a picture of a woman in a high-collared blue dress painting a landscape at an easel. Over everything lay that all too noticeable atmosphere of the sick-chamber, created by a scatter of bowls and jugs and towels and the fug of lingering, invincible illness.

The girl sat propped up against the pillows, while her mother busied herself with straightening the rucked blankets and tucking down the edge of the sheet. She was not much older than Carlotta, perhaps only about twenty-two, but pain and weakness had hollowed themselves into her features and given them a false maturity, as if the process of ageing had redoubled its swiftness so as to achieve its work in time. Her hair hung in lank curls across the frayed bordering of the old woollen shawl covering her nightgown. Smiling wanly, she stretched out a hand towards Carlotta, who did not move towards the bed but stood there trembling and awkward as the girl shifted herself into a more comfortable position for receiving us.

'Mother's told me how nice you are to her, signorina. If I'd known you were coming to visit I'd have asked her to wake me earlier, only . . .'

She broke off in a fit of coughing, cramming a bit of sheet into her mouth to gag its dry rattle. Then, as if this had shaken her into some sort of momentary life, she leaned forward across the bedclothes, her glance sombre and fervent.

'I'll be well again soon,' she said, the pitch of her voice rising with a queurlous sharpness. 'They told me it's nothing serious, just to rest.' Tilde, her back turned to us, was measuring something from a bottle on to a spoon and clinking it into a glass of water. 'And Mother brought me these cherries. Not to eat, of course; I couldn't eat anything like that, not just now. She wanted me to see the colour.' The girl's eyes consumed us, embers of wasted energy and desire. 'They're such a beautiful colour. Then tomorrow she'll bring them back. Or perhaps better tonight. Yes, tonight's better. But aren't they so beautiful?'

The three of us stood for a moment transfixed, as she twisted herself round to contemplate the cherries. There indeed they were, the gleaming carmine *marasche*, some perfectly round, others slightly flattened and lopsided like little pumpkins, with nothing to suggest that they had been touched since Tilde had spirited them into her old carpet-bag that afternoon. The weakening light through the window gave them a spurious polish, as if they had been rolled out of clay. Then Carlotta began to cry.

I've never heard a woman cry like that. Most women weep in the way they laugh, in a sequence of little gasps. When Carlotta burst into tears it was with great choking heaves, the stifled, inchoate utterances of a language she wanted to remember. Staggering towards the bed-end, she held on to one of its finials as though she were drowning and stood there swaying within the surge of her emotions. After a while Tilde came and put a motherly arm around her, but she kept on in a wordless fury of sobbing, voiding herself till she could no longer know who she was. At last she broke free of Tilde and threw herself across the bed, so that the sick girl was able, wonderingly to comfort and caress her, murmuring: 'There now, there, don't cry, oh don't,' as Carlotta heaved herself free of her wretchedness.

Giorgi, all this time, had not stirred. When I turned to look at him, I was startled by the extraordinary expression of peevishness mingled with contempt clouding his face. He was not, as I was, a spectator, absorbed by the novelty of everything, but a participant whose impatient disgust heightened the moment's charge of feeling. I saw Tilde too glance at him, with a hint almost of fear. In the white fleshiness from which his eyes bulged black and unrelenting, he looked positively middle-aged.

Suddenly raw and graceless, Carlotta sat up, staring about her as if she hadn't the least notion where she was. Then, reaching awkwardly towards the sick girl, she held her in an embrace. Of course that made the poor creature cough, at which Carlotta seemed almost ready to cry again, exclaiming wretchedly: 'I'm sorry, I'm sorry.'

Her hair had come loose on one side, and as she busied herself with pinning it up, Tilde said: 'You'll be wanting to take the cherries, signorina. I'll find a basket.'

'Oh no, truly, keep them if you wish,' said Carlotta. Giorgi's eyes looked glassier than ever.

'They're ours,' said the girl, smiling ruefully; 'I couldn't eat them even if I wanted. Mother just thought I'd like the colour. You mustn't be angry with her.'

Carlotta made a little indulgent gesture as if to say that it was all forgotten, and Tilde came back into the room with a grubby-looking basket, in which she carefully settled the bowl of cherries. Then she went round the bed, tucking her daughter back in and arranging the pillows, while the sad, paper-faced girl stared at us as if our very going would kill her. Carlotta noticed it while she put on her hat, and went and sat on the bed once more and took her hands and murmured things about coming back and getting well. We went out again through the cavernous monastic passages of the house, this time without dawdling to glance into the room with the piano and the dancers or at the capering nymphs in the painting and the slouching watchers from the balustrade in their petticoats and chemises.

Seeing us to the wicket gate, Tilde seemed to have grown in stature and was scarcely recognisable as the frayed, mousy thing of her former incarnation. Her face, as she watched us out into the square, wore a profoundly satisfied look, as if our intrusion had settled something until then in doubt. With a little smile and a bob to Carlotta she shut the gate behind us and we stood alone in the failing light of early evening.

On the way home, I remember, we were silent until we reached the bottom of the hill, just before the turn that led down to my uncle's house. Here Carlotta halted us and said quietly: 'You know, don't you, that when we get home I am going to say nothing about all this. And that you aren't to say anything either, not even if they ask you. It is to be our secret.'

We nodded with a grave sense of relief that was almost like gratitude.

'You were carrying the cherries.'

'Was I?' said Giorgi wearily. 'Even if I wasn't, it still seems more consistent with your part of the story. Did we eat them after that?' He laughed. 'Oh no, of course we didn't, did we, because we had to eat that wretched cake of Geltrude's. Was I very angry?'

'Not very, not at that,' I said, 'but there is one more bit I can recall.'

Giorgi yawned. The café was nearly empty and the waiters were starting to assume a homegoing impatience.

'What was that?'

'It was when we'd both gone to bed. I pretended to go to sleep, because I didn't want to talk to you. Actually I felt rather sad, thinking about Carlotta. She seemed to me in much more of a pickle than Tilde's poor dying daughter. So I lay there pretending to sleep and thinking about it all. AcFter a while I realised you weren't asleep either. Then I heard you get out of bed, open the door, go along the landing and downstairs. It must have been about one o'clock in the morning and everyone else in the house was tucked up for the night.

'I got up and followed you along the landing. Everything was hot and still, I remember, and I was frightened lest you'd hear the floorboards creak, so I stopped halfway down the stairs and watched you go alone into the hall. The study door was open and your father had left the electric lamp switched on, so that its glow fell on the bowl of cherries Carlotta had told you to put back on the table. And you stood there with your back to me, Giorgi, and I heard you distinctly.'

He turned his astonished face towards me. 'What do you mean, you heard me?'

'I heard you,' I said, 'and you were counting them to see that none was missing.'

La Dolce Prospettiva

The sacristan had begun to think about shutting the church. Visitors that morning had been few – two American boys with spectacles and large bottoms, a German and his wife who had asked unanswerable questions about the pavement, a party of French schoolteachers, and the usual handful of old women from the neighbourhood who came to mumble through the Rosary in the cosy half-darkness. Somewhere down there in the gloom sat mad Agnese, whispering her litany of filth to the crowned Madonna she had abused daily for forty years since her lover had been killed by a partisan bullet a day or two after she had caught him cheating on her with a dressmaker from Mestre. They called her Agnese Casso – *casso* being Venetian for 'cock' – because that was her favourite among the words she whispered to the Madonna. You heard her going 'cock ... cock ... fucking cock ... screw you ... screw your fucking cock', while the Madonna looked down at her with that expression of elegant, slightly distasteful forbearance the sculptor had given her in perpetuity.

This was the only church in Venice with electric candles. In front of each altar, each image and crucifix, stood a little cluster of bulbs ranged in two rows like the nipples of a sow, protruding from white plastic tubes with simulated drops of wax falling down their sides. The priest, obsessed with neatness, was proud of them because they made no mess and could be doused at the flick of a switch, but the sacristan privately held there to be something vulgar in such expedient meanness and felt ashamed by the dripping prodigality of adjacent parishes, where every painting and statue was wreathed in an aura of tremulous, uneven flame.

They had argued about this, as they had now begun arguing about the mice behind the high altar. The sacristan had grown rather fond of the mice; he was not quite as far as giving them names, but their fearlessness became a comfort to him as he pottered about in the presbytery. The priest, on the other hand, was mystified by what they could possibly find to live on, and he took this as his excuse to ordain that they should go. It had not come to an open refusal on the sacristan's part to set traps or put down poison, but he hoped that simply by ignoring Don Fabio's instructions he might be able succinctly to make a point in their favour.

Rolling away the carpet, he swept a little scatter of their black droppings from the step. His back had started to hurt, an infallible clock which told him it was nearly closing time. For a moment he rested his broom against the extended marble foot of the kneeling angel at one side of the altar and looked up at the longs trip of canvas on the wall above him, depicting the Rest on the Flight into Egypt. Mostly he could not understand why people came to look at the pictures in the church, for they seemed to him impossibly gloomy and ugly. It was even less easy to comprehend why the three huge paintings of the childhood of Christ surrounding the presbytery should be thought of so little account, since quite clearly they were the handsomest of all. He didn't so much care for Mary and Joseph and the Infant Jesus, who inhabited all three, but the figures around them, the knotty-fisted, wattle-necked old men, the beggars with their ragged beards, the soldiers in plumed helmets and leather aprons, and the women clutching children to their great glistening paps and splaying their livid white thighs as if to fall on top of him, these he never tired of staring at.

There was one altarpiece everyone wanted to see, whose appeal had always mystified him. It stood above an altar halfway up the north side of the church, equipped with one of those timed lights operated by dropping a 500-lire coin into a box. An exceedingly celebrated master had depicted a trio of saints standing on ornate marble steps, below which crouched a consort of cherubs playing stringed instruments, with a mountain landscape stretching away in the distance.

It seemed to the sacristan a very dreary piece of work. A few years ago they had taken the picture away for cleaning, and put in its place a cheerful, buxom Saint Helen sharing her joy at the Invention of the True Cross with several expensively garbed ladies-in-waiting. Therefore he greeted the original picture's return with something like annoyance. Its colours were maybe a little brighter, and some discreet swabbing had disclosed, in the panel's lower left corner, a majolica pot of irises and carnations which, according to Don Fabio, had excited the attention of scholars, though the sacristan wondered why they should bother their heads over such things. In this old picture Saint Catherine looked cross and frumpish, Saint Anthony's face was almost lost in a hood and a grubby beard, and Saint Sebastian, stuck with two or three token arrows, had the insolent, smirking assurance of those blond deckhands from Chioggia who work the boats on the Grand Canal.

When the door at the west end of the church was pushed open and a man and a woman came in, the sacristan was sardonically unsurprised at seeing them moving round behind the nave pillars towards this same altar. Taking up the broom and leaning on it, he peered at them from his vantage point on the steps. They were foreigners, you could tell by their age, elderly Italians never came looking at pictures like this. The man was tall and stooping, with a pencil-sharp nose and thick, rimless spectacles, dressed in a pale grey suit. The sole eccentricity in the woman's appearance was provided by a pair of bright green stockings, oddly at variance with the nun-like sobriety of her navy-blue dress.

From her money nuns might have built themselves a

cathedral. It was what made her believe, at the outset of their friendship, that her companion, a historian of Renaissance art garlanded with honours by a score of universities and half a dozen museums, was simply interested in soliciting her potential bounty. She had not reckoned on the subtler, more enduring fascination her wealth possessed for him or on his cogent suggestions as to its intelligent disposal. To her, then, was given the merit of having enabled one civic gallery to snaffle a brace of Guercinos, endued with all the lyrical opulence of the artist's final manner, and another to secure the Vigée-Lebrun portrait of Lafayette's niece which had been so hotly pursued by a private buyer in Switzerland.

Yet he so consistently wasn't, she perceived, a mere fundraiser. What absorbed him was the peculiar frame of affluence in which she and others like her moved. He'd developed an entire system of argument – casuistry, some might have called it – to acquit the rich of those more banal accusations flung at them by envy and indigence. Neither snobbish nor greedy, he appeared to enjoy her company for what it was, that of a sensible woman, patient and informed, whose qualities were immeasurably enhanced by the easy assumptions money allowed her to make.

She had liked the professor from the first. His face bore the lines and marks of old America, of the patrician enlightenment which had planted New England with libraries and institutes, odeons and athenaeums, in an unshakeable confidence (that somehow wasn't vanity) as to the ultimate rightness of its considered discriminations. Something essentially Protestant in him perversely appealed to her, a Baltimore Catholic with lace-curtain Irish grandparents. His manner, dry, questioning, pragmatic, was so entirely alien that she longed to acquire it for herself, as though by continuing association it might rub on to her in miraculous transference like the bloom of a tree.

There was a husband, living with ruthless discretion in New York and sedulously never asking her how she spent these precious weeks in Europe, who had taken the trouble all the same to ascertain that with a companion of this kind both his wife and her assets were entirely safe. The single moment of cynical amusement yielded by his researches came in discovering that she had rivals. The widow of a cement millionaire, who expected her servants to pack everything in a shade of tissue paper calculated to 'sympathise' with the article in question, whisked the paragon off every April to look at Burgundian abbeys or to explain Goya to her in Madrid, while another museum patroness was of such immaculate wealth that on a single autumn weekend in Florence her two secretaries were installed at the Excelsior while she and her maid retreated to a villa on the heights of Bellosguardo.

Perhaps this impressed the professor, though the husband, having met him on more than one occasion, was hardly disposed to believe it. He was not insensitive to the possibility that his wife might have attractions of an altogether different kind from those which had originally captivated him, but he still found it perplexing that someone of the professor's apparent self-assurance, such entire conviction in his own worth, should submit, even for so short a time, to being not much more than a tour guide, or at best one of those guest lecturers featuring on the schedules of Mediterranean cruises 'for the informed traveller'.

What sort of information, in the end, did she require? Her husband, tending to see every aspect of knowledge in terms of a commodity, was puzzled as much by the depth of her suddenly awakened wish to know as by the desire itself. Was she perhaps intending to write a book? Had she a grand collection in view? The notion of her indulging a detached curiosity was no more convincing to him than it would have been to her. Long ago, with a lonely, intractable resolution whose force took her initially by surprise, she had abandoned curiosity for the simpler prompting of desire.

Under this imperative she met, or more precisely engaged,

the professor for their annual trysts, which generally took place in the spring and summer in cities of her naming. He never demurred. why not must be obvious. She'd grown used, with an increasing pang of acknowledgement, to his grand grey head, its hair parted with a certain residual boyishness, the spectacles always unrimmed above the slightly disdainful nose, waiting there for her in the various apologetic little sheds of the private airports at which her plane landed. And in the long interim between meetings, she sustained a careful correspondence with him on questions of art. 'I have been thinking over what you said about Giambologna' or 'Your article on Primaticcio reached me yesterday' or 'It struck me that the Corots we saw in the gallery at Reims were probably . . .' her letters began, and he would reply to them point by point in his clear, stalking hand, with a patience she was sure he had never exercised towards his students.

She was careful, of course, not to pester him with too many letters. In that way she could ensure that his answers, when these arrived, would be long enough for her to feel that she might discover something else wrapped within their lines, some earnest of a hoped-for declaration. For Giambologna and Primaticcio were not honestly the matters at issue, however much, in more shamelessly self-deceptive moods, she might have persuaded herself of the contrary. He must at last, she reasoned, discern her meaning and applaud her reticence in not forcing it upon him except by this sublest of stratagems. Perhaps they'd even laugh about it. She was almost certain of his indulgence whenever she should pluck up the courage to speak, but in the end the sign, that little nod of assent which allowed for her to go forward, must be his.

Periodically she had rehearsed the details of the occasion as she imagined it might be. The backdrop was along the lines of some sparely hung, roomy modern gallery in a German art city or of the walls around some hilltop *borgo* above the upper Tiber where the pair of them would be admiring the view. And at the acceptable time, by whatever mysterious impulse the time should come to seem acceptable, the professor would turn, that was all, without necessarily saying anything, and from so simple a movement she could take her cue. She'd say something in itself dreadfully banal and without half its intended force, to which in his devastatingly clear yet never especially resonant voice, establishing authority over her in an introductory climb out of its deepest register, he could give the inelectably coherent answer.

Though several opportunities had presented themselves, she believed, or was disposed to believe, that each must have been spoiled by some unseasonable intrusion, frustrating his delicate impulse at the crucial moment. The time so far had never seemed quite acceptable. At Pommersfelden they had been interrupted by the gardener's dog, in the Camera degli Sposi an officious custodian had pressed them to leave because a Belgian television crew needed the space for filming, and at the Petit Trianon a party of schoolchildren had burst in almost as if they knew exactly what they were disturbing.

Would it have been better if he'd managed to be vulgar or embarrassing? His whole life, she was certain, strenuously propelled itself in the opposite direction. Everybody said women were uninteresting to him 'in that way', but his little assiduities when they were together suggested that her influence might be something else entirely. She knew such people of course and how they behaved, but the gossip about him was easy enough to dismiss. Behind his attentions, what was more, lay no obviously cynical calculation. There'd never been the least suggestion of him pricing her, as it were, for acquisition. What seemed instead to engage him was something like an anthropological exercise, observing her as part of a species which, however familiar it was to him through background and upbringing, had never lost its fascination, and delighting in what he saw.

Yesterday evening there had been signs which encouraged her. For whatever reason, Venice on this occasion was making the professor strangely emotional. Emotional for him, whose only apparent access of strong feeling was a certain sulky annoyance when the conversation at dinner became too trifling or when he was forced into social contact with people for whom advancing age made him feel he could not spare the time. Here, suddenly, he had begun doing things she would never have supposed him capable of, acting on the sort of innocent impulses he might have had – though she could hardly believe it – when, as a youth on his first visit, he had gone to look at the Carpaccios in the Scuola di San Giorgio. He made her halt, for instance, on top of the Accademia Bridge purely in order to ask her whether this were not the most exhilarating prospect in Venice. She agreed politely that it was, but the behaviour still seemed out of character, the response too broad and general, almost to banality. When they walked into the church of the Salute to look at the Titian, the professor had paused and very deliberately unfastened the left cuff button of his shirt. Yesterday during lunch at the hotel he had surprised the waiter, and astonished her, by asking for a cup of camomile tea. When it arrived, he left it untouched, puzzling her still further by saying as they got up to leave: 'I wonder which of us ordered tea?'

She'd heard about people going mad in Venice. Assiduously preparing before setting off from New York, she came across the story of George Eliot's husband, who threw himself into the Grand Canal on their honeymoon, apparently in a fit of depression. The possibility that something similar might be happening to the professor was altogether less congenial than the idea of him steeling himself for some sort of admission, an intimate truth declared whose sudden candour must seem the more valuable for being so untypical of him.

This morning, when the hotel launch took them down the canal beside the Arsenale and they had walked through that agreeable snatch of what he called 'popular Venice', under the washing lines and trilling canaries of the *calli* and *campielli* west of San Martino (nothing, he pronounced, worth looking at there except for a rather childish Girolamo da

Santa Croce) – this morning wasn't one she had specifically assigned for the moment of unburdening. Yet whether it was a sympathy in their apprehensions of the place itself, the shared capacity for reading an intricate text of walls, doorways and paving stones, or whether it was a sense that here, more than anywhere else in Venice except among some dismal clutter of tenements up by Canareggio or in the grass-grown alleys beyond Angelo Rafaele, they were safe from inquisitive scrutiny, she'd begun to perceive the time's imperious fitness.

The façade of the church, white as they approached it, with its little ridges and scoops like the surface of a body, gave her an unfamiliar courage. She was not specially brave, and much of her energy and expenditure in recent years had been devoted to finding ways of avoiding threatened embarrassment, so that by now her ordinary course of existence seemed effectively fenced in against the intrusions of what she was in the habit of calling 'unpleasantness', a word whose imprecision comprehended a whole variety of social and practical fears. Now, however, this bold marble frontage, buffed to glistening ivory by the restorers whose wooden *impalcatura* had only lately been taken down, looked like the very stuff of certainty, so that when they came up immediately under its shadow she almost pushed the professor through the curtain into the gloom beyond. And for the first time, when he began to discourse on the wonders of the painting they'd come specifically to see, she stopped listening and looked round furtively instead at the line of side chapels with their stucco festoons and chequered pavements, down the aisle formed by ranked chairs towards the doorway and its adjoining postcard-stand beside a forlorn little heap of *Famiglia Cristiana*, and at the crowned Madonna, under whose disclaiming arms, those of an actress gracefully implying her own unworthiness in the face of rapturous applause at the end of the show, sat an old woman muttering in tones less of devotion than of barely suppressed rage.

'... began it in 1506,' the professor was saying, 'after his return from Padua, where he'd been executing a commission for Pietro Minola, a humanist scholar and collector. There was a perfectly ridiculous article in the *Burlington* by Randall suggesting that it was meant to be an attonement for the profanity of Minola's painting – *Rape of Proserpine*, you'll have seen it in Chicago – but I wrote pointing out that Langenbach, as long ago as 1928, had deciphered the Greek inscription on the column-base at the left of the canvas as implying that the whole thing was intended allegorically.'

He had that English or at least un-American way of speaking she so admired but would never have sought to imitate, with its use of emphatic adverbs, 'perfectly', 'utterly', 'absolutely', and ideas of a sentence as a free-growing verbal tree shooting out unpredictable subordinate branches. Ordinarily she relished listening in the guise of a favourite student taking notes, as it were, and her capacity for remembering the minutest details of his exegesis was, she knew, hugely flattering. Today she simply wanted him to finish, an unworthy wish that he should get on with it starting to fret at the edges of her traditionally composed absorption. 'Now,' she thought, 'let it be now,' as if the most logical process in the world must have been for him to break off his lapidary assessment of a Renaissance altarpiece in order to disclose what she imagined were his authentic feelings.

In fact the professor had never believed in substituting the emotions aroused in him by others for the peculiar kind of truth accorded to his sensibilities by a picture or a statue. Though he didn't initially intend his Upper East Side apartment as a sequence of small galleries, each with its visual *clou* pinning together the rest of the collection like an eyecatcher as the resolution of a formal landscape, this was the way in which the place had turned out, and he was frankly entranced by the result. Looking around at the cabinet of French Baroque medals, the two Delacroix drawings, the small Savoldo portrait of a young man, the Bouchardon bust of Mme de Lancenet, the rose-patterned Kirman prayer rug given him by a grateful scholar who had arrived at the museum as a refugee from Hungary, he would acknowledge, to himself and occasionally to others, that these mattered more than the people he invited to sit among them. And from something outrageous, a deliberate flouting of conventional pieties, the repeated assertion of this principle grew into an article of faith, securing him against any more of those fruitless dramas of attachment he had allowed himself to play out during his boyhood and youth.

From time to time he'd tried to remind his friend – self-protectively he thought of her as a friend – of this reality as it had now become, but something always unsettled him in her insistent willingness to understand, as if perception were less important than the more general indulgence which gave it room. Since she wanted to know merely so as to possess, he wasn't inclined to deliver more than the occasional discreet warning.

Wouldn't it in any case have been horrifying to her, this rationale of coldness and distance, in which marble grew more palpable than flesh, and the gesso and gilding of a picture-frame defined the object of feeling more authentically than all the attempts in the world at physical description and character portrayal? For several years now the professor had solaced himself with a collection of adult videos ordered discreetly from catalogues sent to him under plain cover at the museum. The scenarios were nearly always the same: a young man named Brad or Chuck or Todd happened on another boy with a similar name who was mending a car or painting the house or putting a step on the front porch, and the pair, adjourning to the bedroom, began a vigorously episodic enactment of sex, in which the varied sequence of camera angles always reminded him of an architect's portfolio, front and back elevations, side views, floor plans, etcetera. The coupling, which might be elaborated by the chance arrival of a third youngster, needing no persuasion to undress, ended in what, so the professor learned, was known

as 'the money shot', an exuberant orgasm artificially pro-
longed via multiple repetitions of the same cinematic instant
in which pearl-hued curlicues of sperm bounced across the
screen like the explosions of a Roman candle.

The point of the whole enterprise, it seemed to the professor, was that there should be as little sense as possible
of the participants becoming emotionally involved with one
another. Chuck never got to kiss Todd, and there was no
suggestion that after the various stages of sexual commerce
had reached their culmination Todd would fix a future date
with Brad. Most satisfying of all was the almost total absence
of adumbrative plot detail or connecting dialogue. The videos
with which friends from Europe supplied him were notably
tiresome in this respect: far too much emphasis was laid on
context and scene-setting, with coy little location shots and
incipits deliberately, intended to dampen the viewer's excited
expectations. They were like old-fashioned novels with
sequential stories and generous helpings of 'atmosphere',
when his preference in this case was entirely for the kind of
modernist fictions in which nothing happens, character and
moral development are unimportant and all that matters is
discourse and subtext.

What he liked in the American videos was the way in which
the conversational element was so consistently suppressed.
Though the concomitant moans and gasps of sexual engagement were as essential to establishing its genuineness as the
diversified slants adopted by the filmmaker, anything in
the way of actual words was scarcely audible. You could
see the boys' lips move, catch them muttering colloquial
exchanges of a few words each, yet the idea of anyone establishing a personal identity under such circumstances was
completely alien to the rigid conventions of the genre.

The professor enjoyed it thus. Brad and Todd, near-voice-
less, denying any perspective beyond what their simulated
coupling suggested, had a gratifying integrity of the sort
which transcended arguments about provenance, dating and

attribution. Looking now at Saint Sebastian, a figure whose nakedness was rendered unembarrassing by a pair of pleated white drawers neatly tied below the navel with a string, he felt a curious frisson of doubt. It wasn't that his faith in the painting itself was shaken, simply that this was another of those twinges with which, in recent days, his capacity for emotion had begun surprising him. Of course, Venice could have had something to do with it, though there were things in Florence and Rome which must always have meant far more to him. Through a mere coincidence the place, it seemed to him now, was the backdrop against which a set of impure commonplaces had begun their subversive assault on his composure, iron-willed, selfish, stiffened by the unassailable rightness of an aesthetic judgement to which others bowed as to some numinous decree.

He knew perfectly well what this woman wanted him to say, but her desire held no significance beside this displacement of his comfortable egoism with a sudden sequence of vistas, whence he could dimly perceive a *dramatis personae* of past attachments and half-effected longings moving forward to reclaim him. If any of these moved their lips, then the words they spoke must soon grow pitilessly clear. Beyond loyalty and the vague generic admiration for her taste and intelligence he was always ready to acknowledge in public, he felt no more for her than for the old creature down there barking filth at the impassively smiling Madonna. 'Shit, you're full of shit, that's what you are, full of it, shit, fucking shit!' The inexorable harshness of the reiterated words, which a charitable impulse might interpret simply as an alternative form of prayer, broke in upon the gathering bewilderment of the professor's self-absorption, and he realised that they had been standing there for several minutes without saying anything.

'I'm afraid the natural light's very poor,' he said, covering his embarrassment by dropping another coin into the box. 'You need to move a little further back to get the best view

– as long as you don't mind me talking over my shoulder to you.'

'Not at all,' he heard her whisper, and wondered how, when at last he should have to turn round, he was going to confront the fact of her disappointment. Would she start to cry, or, still worse, assume the sort of cold bravado which placed a formal distance between them? He needed at all events to talk, to obviate those possible meanings she might attribute to his silence. If everything else failed, he could always blame the sacristan, hovering near the high altar in his dustcoat like a grubby beetle, and beginning to rattle his keys for a warning that the church was about to close.

So the professor began again, talking this time about the architecture of the balustraded platform on which the three saints stood, about Saint Anthony's black pig and the singular botanical exactness of Saint Catherine's palm of martyrdom and the relationship of the angel playing a viol in the left foreground to a seated goddess in an antique cameo known to have been bought by the painter in 1498 from the Anconetan merchant Ciriaco Podesti – 'who, by the way, is not to be confused with Cyriac of Ancona'.

Yet none of these were the words he wanted to say. Venice had confused him here too, he perceived, as much as it muddled the sad, patient woman standing now at his shoulder, waiting on her implausible moment. The difference between them was that he knew, as she did not, the place's fatal gift for corroding every smallest attendant faculty of self-control. To talk about ascriptions and attributions, the warfare of iconographers and hermeneuticists, was more than simply a professional grace with which he chose to oblige her as a condescension to wealth and enlarged aesthetic discernment. He heard himself speaking now, of the hills in the distance up which minute figures spurred horses and drove cattle, of the peculiar relationship of the cloud formations to those it was possible to see on certain days overhanging the city, of the extraordinary precision with which the painter had rendered Saint Sebastian's feet, and acknowledged, in this detachment for his own grave, low voice, exact in its enunciations, a little merciless as he knew she liked him to be, that he was mortally afraid.

That's what they meant, those little rushes of emotion he had experienced yesterday like the lifting of a breeze, those sudden attempts at re-enacting things done forty years before, when, as a diffident young sophomore in a blazer and neatly buffed Oxfords, he'd been 'introduced' at Palazzo Barbaro and spent an afternoon of acute discomfort in a bathing costume under an umbrella at the Lido, between sprinting indecorously to Santa Maria Formosa to see the Palma Vecchio, devoting four pages of Piazzesi's best letter-paper to a bejewelled, Pateresque description of Catena's *Martyrdom of Saint Christina* and resolving to rehabilitate Alessandro Vittoria in a brace of lapidary articles for the *Art Journal*.

Vance, the friend to whom he had written so gushingly about Catena, was a painter whose work he'd pretended to admire at a gallery vernissage in Manhattan purely so that he might get to talk to him. In truth the style, so candid and specific in its celebrations of unguarded maleness, had seemed to him quite embarrassingly vulgar, but he never told Vance this because, on arriving home at his aunt's brownstone on East 75th, he realised that somewhat inopportunely he'd fallen in love.

The point, of course, was to say nothing about this to Vance, which seemed easy enough, since he was married, something the young man discovered on his second telephone call. 'I'm his wife,' said a woman's voice, and then – by which he was wholly taken aback – 'Oh, of course, you couldn't have known. He'll be so happy you called.' Her assumption that she knew how Vance would feel in response to him telephoning was disconcerting, the more so because he was discomfited at his own importunity, and wondered why anybody else should be made happy by it. Named Justina, she was half-Brazilian, one of those handsomely scaled, appetising women whom painters marry with the apparent idea of painting nobody else afterwards. Vance had not followed this rule, but the studio traffic of men invited to model for the self-consciously poetic friezes and mythopoeic ensembles on which his imagination insisted – so monotonously, thought the professor, who, though not a professor quite yet, already threatened to be professorial – never dinted her composure. all she did was laugh quietly, not at them exactly but scarcely with them, and make voluminous, episodic dinners to which they were always bidden to stay.

Never in the world would he have taken off his clothes for Vance, but he was welcome nevertheless in that long room, the ascetic brightness of it accentuated by the clumps of stacked canvases against its bare walls. Close to the door, always unlocked, lay a kitchen in which somebody, not necessarily always Justina, could be heard fixing coffee or preparing a meal, as if this were some sound effect essential to the *tout-ensemble* of the studio. At the further end, a distance impossible for him to cover without suddenly feeling vulnerable and afraid, there would be Vance sketching and chatting comfortably with the unembarrassed Otis or Wilbur or Frank of the moment, whose proportions the professor was invited to admire.

The unbuttoned nature of everything was, he knew, designed to test him, and it was a foregone conclusion that he would fail. Almost certain that Justina had witnessed ordeals of this kind before, yet equally convinced that their parabolic outline wasn't something she specifically desired, he'd half made up his mind to engage her on the subject at some moment when the two of them were alone. The nakedness of the man, whoever he was, sprawled in an armchair, leaning on a plaster column-drum, standing hands on hips in the glare of a photographer's floodlight so that Vance could get an exact fall of shadow among the abdominal muscles, was strangely unerotic, a footnote to the far more complex challenge flung in his direction by the painter himself. He wondered how many others had been similarly taunted – for the whole thing was in the end scarcely more than that – and what in each case provided the breaking point.

For him it arrived one morning in early summer when, maddened by a sequence of trifling engagements that had kept him from going to the studio for almost a week, he abandoned the composition of some dismissive but heavily referenced paragraphs on Sano di Pietro and set off fretfully towards the West Village. Pushing open the door – never locked unless both of them were out – he was taken aback at first by the general silence. The kitchen was empty and a naked live male no longer routinely completed the perspective down the length of the studio. On the old cane daybed in one corner, among a tumble of cushions and rugs, Vance lay sound asleep.

For the first time unafraid to cross the intervening emptiness, the professor moved resolutely towards him, pausing only when near enough to touch. Vance's lips, between the close-trimmed beard, were slightly open, and the oily mop of brown curls trailing around his face gave him the look of a drowned man some capricious wave might have hoisted on to a ledge of rock. One arm was thrown back over the cushions. The whiteness of it against the dingy grey singlet he wore was as mesmerising in its immediacy as the fronds of brown hair bushing in its hollow like something that had taken root among stones. The casual acknowledgement of a truth, made not so much by the defencelessness of Vance's sleeping form as by this single feature of his outstretched arm, was what rooted the professor to the spot. In a moment the vault under that span of bone and sinew and flesh had become, as it were, the place within which he knew who he was. Just then Vance, opening his eyes, sat up, rubbing the sleep off his face.

'We're going to Fire Island when Justina gets back from marketing,' he said, as if he'd known all along who would be there looking at him. 'Want to come?' Utterly mortified, the young man said nothing. A slow smile of recognition crept across Vance's features. 'You ever been to Fire Island, Jerry?'

Once on the street, where he'd been terrified of running into Justina, who'd have wanted to bring him back again, a recaptured fugitive, he raced towards the avenue to hail a taxi and let it carry him, nerveless, uptown. When he got to his aunt's house he banged the street door so loudly on entering that the maid, watering the ferns in the hall, exclaimed 'My, Mr Jerome!' as he hurried to the study and began a yet more virulent denunciation of the wretched Sano.

Since then there'd been nobody like Vance to unsettle him; he had made sure of that. The succession of lovers, anointed by his patronage, had all been neat, clean boys who wore neckties and brushed their shoes and knew how to offer exquisite apologies in writing for the dinner engagements they were forced to miss. With a positively parental satisfaction he had seen them settled, one by one, into graceful tenure of curatorships or ensconced in the creditable comfort of those discreet advisory positions which required them from time to time to authenticate a style or declare a distinguished provenance. One or two of them even married, not always in the name of mere respectability.

Such a detail was in no sense painful. He was glad instead to have given them the defining rock or tree or cloud which should fix their scale and proportion. And they in their turn surrounded him as elegant markers of that private landscape of deference from whose enclosure he occasionally struck out in glacial contempt at the folly and vulgarity of his fellow art historians. It was his solace now to contemplate these boys of his scattered so opportunely across the map of America, David in Chicago, Philip in Cleveland, Merritt in Pittsburgh, Bruce at the Kimbell, Larry at the Hungtington, the sleek-napped, tight-buttoned foot soldiers he had drilled with such lethal astuteness in the discipline of scholarly annihilation, with the artillery of envenomed footnotes amid a stout emplacement of bibliography.

Why was it then that at this moment these acolytes seemed so fatally to have abandoned him, when one or other of them might have stood guard, as on earlier occasions, against . . . well what, if not the silently importunate presence at his shoulder, towards whom he dared not turn? Perhaps against solitude, something he had taken care should never trouble him except at routine morning hours of self-imposed quiet among his books. Or likelier still, against the inchoate terror solitude occasioned, stealing up on him as it had done so insidiously here in Venice, when he could not plead an actual loneliness in defence of his vulnerability.

With the desperation of a hand clinging to the edge of a precipice, his gaze fixed itself once more upon the trio of saints, and he began talking about the hagiography surrounding Catherine of Alexandria and the way in which it had led to the theory, first propounded by an English dilettante named Burrell (and here he allowed himself a little fling at the British love-affair with amateurism), that the figures represented the three principal phases of human adulthood. Yet what he really saw, what wholly transfixed him because he had been fearful of recognising it before, was a solitary detail in the pose of that smirking Saint Sebastian, so gracefully the martyr in his pleated linen drawers. For while the saint's left hand was placed negligently against his hip, the right arm was raised to grasp the arrow shaft jutting from his lower neck, thus exposing the contour of sinew and flesh where the limb articulated with the shoulder. Vance lay sleeping again among the tumbled cushions of the daybed that afternoon in the studio, as vulgarly palpable in the grey singlet which rose and fell to the soundless level of his breathing as the professor's own desire, startled and immense, to which the upstretched arm with its thick tuft of hair beneath gave a logical summons. 'Now,' the young man had heard the blood murmur, 'now.'

A hustling, insistent vividness in this pseudo-epiphany rubbed out everything else. Of course, it had meant to all the time, the professor realised. The botched experience stood at his shoulder like an assassin, so that he forgot now who was behind him, at that spot on the chapel step where the light from the half-moon window should not pester their view of the canvas. To the woman waiting for him to finish and say what she thought he must, the suddenly opening distance across the scaled marble towards him was beyond measuring. How small both of them looked, though the sacristan, starting to jangle his keys again in polite warning as the church clock struck the quarter-hour. From the half-darkness by the door he could hear mad Agnese muttering: 'Cock ... cock ... screw you ... face full of shit!'

You shouldn't have, said the Madonna's politely deprecating arms, you really shouldn't, there was honestly no need.

Caliginous

Nobody ever calls us by our real names. For instance, Sprue was christened Francesca – her parents are seriously devout and go to the Oratory every Sunday – but she's been known as Sprue ever since she was at Woldingham. Goodness knows why. Granny says it's something horses get, and that one of the hunters at Braxton actually died of it and they sacked a groom for not calling the vet in time. Anyway, nobody would dream of using the same Francesca unless they were angry with Sprue, which is sort of impossible.

And Teresa's always been known as Sandy. Or at any rate from the time we all lived in Egerton Gardens and she came back from crossing Africa in a sleeping bag and got this beastly red sand everywhere, so that it bunged up the Hoover and some of it got in Hamish's tea and he was hopping. She said we ought to be pleased, as it wasn't just any old sand, it was an authentic bit of the Sahara. So she got called Sandy and it stuck.

Then there's Bunt, whose real name is Sophia; and Charlie, who of course isn't called Charlotte but Alice; and Tricky and El and Tad; and I'm Fudge, which is simple because it's just short for Fiona. Too simple, according to Guy. He says the whole point is that people like us give each other nicknames so that others who don't really belong won't guess who we're talking about. A sort of code, if you like. He says they all did it in Victorian times to prevent inconvenient climbers getting into society. You mentioned a name like Lulu or Jiminy or Skimper, and if someone didn't know who was being referred to, then it meant they weren't quite the thing. Apparently it's got something to do with the solidarity of a class which feels it's under threat.

Anyway that's what Guy says, and you believe him because it's just pointless not to. He's seriously brainy, and a lot of us are rather afraid of him. Being clever like that used to be thought a bit – well, if not exactly common, at any rate slightly off, something to be suspicious about. I remember when Tricky's sister Vim got engaged to a don at Oxford, her parents absolutely checked out his credentials to make sure he was safe, and she only got the family all-clear when they heard he went out with the Heythrop twice a week in the season.

Guy wouldn't hunt if you paid him. He's not deeply anti or anything, just not a country person. We asked him down to Candover one Christmas and he was bored out of his skull, poor lamb. Hated going for walks, wouldn't even try skating when the lake froze over, and had almost nothing to talk about with Boy. Mum said she'd be happy if she never saw him again, gave her the creeps, all lanky and hollow-eyed and brooding, asking questions about when the portraits on the stairs were painted and who put the Chinese wallpaper in the yellow bedroom. Grampy had a blazing row with him about Wagner one evening, almost came to blows over it, because Guy said it was music for fascists and Jew-haters. Grampy didn't like that one bit, and said he hadn't gone all the way through the Normandy landings to be told he was on the side of the Germans just for liking *Lohengrin*.

I suppose they were afraid I'd marry him or something. We were always together, after all, from the moment we started on the antiques course years ago, and we both got the giggles at that ridiculous little number who couldn't pronounce words like 'scagliola' and 'ormolu' but talked in this fraightfly caltiveeted and refeened voice, like someone trying to get a bit of nougat unstuck off their top teeth. There was this amazing moment when he started off on eighteenth-century porcelain by saying: 'Aim a bit more taided ep on this sebjict then wot ai woz last yah.' We *hooted*!

Guy had just come down from Oxford. He narrowly missed a first because he was too flippant at his vivat or whatever it's called, and turned up in his evening clothes after going to somebody's thrash outside Wantage. Of course the dons all had mega chips on the shoulder, so he didn't stand a chance, though one side of him probably yearned for it. His mother was Jewish, you see, and they're always so brainy and neurotic about being thought clever. She killed herself in a hotel in Morocco when Guy was ten. There'd been a lover, some French boy she was besotted with, who wrote poetry and talked to her about philosophy, and they went to this place by the sea called Essaouira, a sort of hang-out for parties, and the French boy and Guy's mother had an absolute godfather of a row and she took an overdose the same night.

Afterwards Guy hated his father. It's what happens with people like that, they always blame the surviving parent, though it isn't necessarily their fault. I could talk about it with him, because he's never kept anything from me. We've told each other everything, or at any rate I've told Guy. He was marvellous after I broke up with Piers Okeover, and a total geezer when my sister was killed. It was like going to a shrink – I've never been to one, but that's what people tell you – only without the guilt. One just lay on the sofa and burbled and sniffled a bit, and Guy listened with his head on one side, in that way he has like a giraffe. Then he started analysing it all, pulling it to and fro and arranging things, as if he'd been tidying it away for me into different drawers. After he'd done this for me over Piers, I went home and wrote the bastard a letter, and Annabel Carbery, top psychobitch from hell, came up to me at a p.v. at the gallery and said: 'Piers wondered whether that letter you sent him was just you taking dictation from Guy.'

She had a point, I suppose. Guy's got a way of saying

things which somehow gets into your conversation, so that you find yourself repeating his ideas down to the very last word. A bit spooky, really, like having a guru or Svengali or something. The only thing you can't possibly repeat is his perfectly appalling stammer. He's tried having it cured, and fell for some dreadful phoney ad by an Indian in Tulse Hill who claimed to do it with mantras, and then had almost complete success from somebody in Worthing who simply got him repeating things and then reciting them by heart and slipping-in bits of conversation.

But it's never totally gone, and sometimes, poor poppet, he's utterly stymied, just standing there snapping his fingers as if the word was about to come running up saying 'sorry I'm late'. When he and Lolo Oliphant and I were all in Spain – and I swear to God this story's true – we got lost in the back of beyond outside Ronda and arrived in this village absolutely ravenous. That wasn't a problem, because in Spain they don't have dinner till somewhere round eleven. Anyway, we all went into this dire-looking place, and a man came out of the back talking Spanish and we simply couldn't understand a word. Lolo did it to A level and her uncle Claud was the ambassador in Buenos Aires, and she'd managed all right up to now, but tonight the systems were down. So the man switched to English and said: 'You wan' dreenk? You wan' eat?' and before either of us could say yes, Guy started snapping his fingers and – no, honestly, I swear – the man burst out laughing and cried: 'Okay, you wan' miou-sseek!' and these other people came out with a guitar and castanets and started to play.

Of course we *hooted*, and once we'd got home Guy told everybody and people thought it was seriously funny. But the funniest bit was a month or two later when he was at a party, and this girl he'd never met before said wasn't it a pity about his stammer and had he ever tried getting it cured and she really must tell him such an amusing story, there were these friends of hers who went to Spain, and one evening blah-di-blah-di-blah. Guy said afterwards that's what he called true fame. He's so good at being able to tell a story against himself, if you see what I mean.

The other night at the Martindales' his stammer was utterly chronic and I knew something must be going on. I always call it the stammerometer, because the more he snaps his fingers the more uptight you know he's getting about things. Hattie Martindale probably noticed it as well. She's so good at things like that. Actually she's insufferably good at every-thing. The Martindales are the sort of people who make you feel mega depressed as soon as you set foot outside their house, they're just too disgustingly perfect. Hattie's a sort of cousin – there's a portrait of Mum's great-aunt Edith in the drawing room at Candover by Herkomer which looks a dead ringer – so I've always been fond of her, but she's the type of family you never need to worry about, you just know they'll never do anything remotely embarrassing or need your support, except for something ordinary like having a baby or someone dying.

You can't imagine Edward Martindale dying. I mean, he will of course, but you honestly can't imagine it. Perhaps that's why we thought he was so boring. I'm not so sure now, but that's what we used to think, 'boring because perfect'. Guy said that, and it summed everything up. And there really wasn't anyone else as far as Hattie was concerned. Well, there'd been a few dreadful boys she met at parties, and a particularly ghastly number who worked for Schroders and drove a Diablo SV and had muscles so big you could see them under his shirt, but Edward was somehow inevitable, knowing about opera and food and getting her tickets for Wimbledon and taking her to Courchevel. Almost a New Man but not so's you'd notice, and a bit vain in the looks department. Well, they both are really. You imagine them giving each other beauty tips, and I know for a fact that they talk about it, because Sprue saw them together in Harvey Nichols buying Clarins Eau Dynamisante and reading the blurb on the box. He's one of those people who never passes a wing-mirror without stopping to see if his hair's tidy. He's got lots of it, like an angel in a fresco. I suppose the thought of running her fingers through it was one of the things which made Hattie keen to marry him. Apart, that is, from the dosh, and the fact that he just seemed to be always miraculously there in ways that most men aren't.

They went to live in Trevor Street in a house that had belonged to Edward's grandparents. Holland Park would have suited them more, but presumably Trevor Street was a convenient arrangement. And handy for Harvey Nichols. We all thought Hattie was going to start sprogging at once but she didn't, and Tricky, who makes a thing out of being deliberately indiscreet, actually asked her why, and she just said they didn't fancy it for the time being. I mean, offhand isn't the word. Bunt and Tommy had barely got down the aisle to the Widor Toccata before they started, and Tad and Christo probably got going before that. If you're seriously into beauty like Edward and Hattie, then babies don't really help, but we did think that after about a year of looking as if somebody had gone over them both with a varnish bottle, preening themselves to death (Guy said – totally brilliant – that it was more a case of airbrush than hairbrush) and getting flawless tans at Edward's parents' house near Forte dei Marmi and making heads turn in the Crush Bar or whenever they walked into Daphne's – we thought Hattie was starting to look a bit grim round the mouth. Not happy. But this time, for some reason, Tricky held back and didn't ask was it babies. I said to Guy I thought it had something to do with Edward's hair, but he didn't seem to find that funny.

Mum noticed it too, when she was staying with Aunt C in Redcliffe Square and the pair of them came round for drinks and the Martindales were here. After they'd gone, Mum said: 'She's quite wrong for him, of course.'

I was gobsmacked, specially when she went on to say: 'He looks at her as though he was looking in the mirror. Women don't respect that sort of thing, do they? You'd have been a much better wife.'

'Oh yeah, thanks a bundle, Mum, marry me off to a man I couldn't respect.'

'Mum doesn't mean that, Fudgie,' said Aunt C, doing her best United Nations peacekeeper bit.

'Never mind what I mean, it's true,' Mum insisted ruthlessly; 'he'd have been serious about you, and he isn't about Hattie.'

'How do you know?'

'I just do. You would too if you had any sense.'

'Mum's only being realistic, Fudgie,' said Aunt C.

Maybe she was, but it made me cross all the same. There was a sort of any-port-in-a-storm feeling about the way they were both saying I should have married Edward, even supposing he was remotely interested in me, which he never was, except as a cousin of Hattie's. I hate the way older people like Mum and Aunt C think you're washed up at twenty-seven if you aren't living in a terrace in Battersea with a banker and a baby. The way they niggle me about it, you'd think hacking it on one's own in a flat in Lincoln Street was like being some frightful old lesbian with a bead necklace and dingle-dangle earrings doing the Chelsea Bohemian bit in the Twenties.

Of course, they still think the sneaky game-plan I've got up my sleeve is to get it together with Guy, 'that Jewish boy with the stutter' as Poppa calls him. You honestly wonder why they can't see he's just not interested in women full stop, but their generation wasn't quite wised up to it like we are, and it certainly wasn't my business to tell them unless they specifically asked. In any case that would only have been more anti-Guy ammo. Aunt C, who's so gung-ho about everything, actually said once that she didn't think gay men – she calls them queers, she's got a funny way of saying it so that it comes out as 'choirs' – she didn't think choirs were really like that, and that all the choirs she knew could have gone straight if they'd found the right woman.

Which of course she and Mum were determined I wasn't going to be. Though now and then I've thought it might be amusing to become Guy's missus, and have one of those marriages where the couple sit in bed and eat chocolates and talk about the men they've both been bonking, while everyone wonders why on earth they stay together and then somebody says: 'But darling, that's the point, don't you see?' Well, it'd be less pointless than the Martindales.

I was thinking about all this the other night before the party. Actually I was thinking about a lot of things, had been for the whole day, silly little fiddly things to do with Poppa letting the shoot to those dodgy Americans, and that business with Boy's tutor, and the drawing some dozy tart brought into the gallery insisting it was a Guardi, and Tad and Christo starting to get wrapped up with the God-botherers at Holy Trinity Brompton, and Sandy announcing she wasn't going to Wexford this year after all, when I was rather hoping to be asked. Everything suddenly seemed so clear and looming at the same time, though I couldn't understand why it was specially now that it all came up, like somebody dredging a lake. It was like I had to have an object to fix worries to. Pathetic, yeah, but that's how it was, and by the time I came home I'd got into a bit of a state. So I lit a cig and made a cup of tea to stop myself going seriously ape. Then I had a nice bath to *The Archers* and got ready to go to Hattie and Edward's.

The car was parked round the corner in Blacklands Terrace, though I needn't have taken it, the evening was so warm. You couldn't see very well, however, as if there was a mist, or just like it had got dark before the light had actually gone. Guy says there's an Italian word for this kind of effect, *caliginoso*. This ferociously glam Italian he tried to have a fling with on the antiques course taught it him, and it became a joke between us after that. We used to talk about all sorts of things being a bit caliginous, but this evening truly was. The edge of the Park behind Knightsbridge Barracks looked so caliginous you might have thought it was the perfect spot for a murder.

Nobody murders anybody in Trevor Street. The houses have that awful just-so feeling to them, there aren't any cracks in the pavement, and everyone's panes are clean. You sort of hope for a few weeds in the window boxes, some puke on the area steps or 'fuck' written in spray-paint over the cream stucco round the door, but you know you'll never get it. It made me feel glum just to ring the bell, and even glummer to walk into the drawing room and see Hattie's smile looking as if it had been fixed for her by one of those people who advertise in the back of *Harper's & Queen.*

Edward was standing at the other end of the room talking to old Fergus Mitchelson, who used to be such a frightful letch until he had his bypass operation. Nowadays he simply leers at one over his bifocals as if to say 'you and me in another life', whereas before one had to make sure one's bum was firmly out of goosing range. For a time I couldn't take my eyes off Edward, he looked so astonishingly different. The hair was all in place, of course, only somehow fluffier, more abundant and rather Victorian-artist-with-floppy-collar, if you know what I mean. But it was his face which really got me. There was a definition to it I hadn't seen before, lean, wolfish, a bit disreputable, totally un-Edward, as if he honestly belonged somewhere a million miles from Trevor Street. No wonder Hattie was looking like the old woman who lived in a vinegar bottle.

Of course, I wanted to talk to Guy about it, and I could see him trying to sempahore at me from the other side of the sofa, but I'd got stuck in a corner with Tad's heavy brother-in-law whose mother's just died of cancer, and you don't want to seem a total heel when people have turned up just for the sake of making a social effort. So I had to listen to why life was better at BZW than Indo-Suez and be exquisitely fascinated by the problems of the Single Currency, when all the time I could see Guy's arms flailing around like a Dutch windmill and hear the stammerometer working overtime. And then to make things worse Bunt and Tommy arrived with the baby, and we all had to go and coo, me especially since I'm its godmother. This is what people do these days, isn't it, arriving late on at a party with a baby, particularly if they know certain people there want them but haven't got them, a sort of nyeeuh-nyeeuh-we've-got-a-baby designer-accessory thing. Hattie must have known this, I felt, because she didn't bat an eyelid and was utterly sweet with Bunt and Tommy for bringing it.

Anyway, this gave me a chance to negotiate the wretched sofa, which had Sandy sitting on it being coruscatingly brilliant to a man from Christie's with freckles about some Baroque bishop's garden she'd discovered in Portugal, and get to Guy, not before time as it seemed. By now he was absolutely whizzing, hardly getting a word out, and the people he was talking to, a couple of Edward's fellow Arburgers, were doing that thing he hates which is helping him to fill in the bits he can't get to. So I just moved in ruthlessly and unhooked him, poor lamb.

'High caliginosity factor tonight, *n'est-ce pas?*' I said, but he didn't pick up on that. Uh-oh, trouble ahead. You could read it in his eyes, great lumps of blackberry jam. I'm never wrong about him. Well, hardly ever.

'F-F-Fudge, I've got to t-t-talk to you about something.'

'Mmm, so I gathered. What doth bug thee, knight-at-arms?'

'There's . . .' He stopped and just stood there snapping his fingers for a moment. 'Are you . . . ? I m-m-mean, will you be g-g-going home afterwards?'

'Sooner or later one does, you know,' I laughed. 'No doubt disgusting old Fergus'd like to whisk me off to the nearest hotel for a quick *à deux*, but oy've got moy stsayndsards, innoy?'

'N-n-no, Fudge, this is serious!' He was getting a shade

hysterical, so I switched off the levity program, and up on the screen came 'sympathetic listener mode'.

'I'm not likely to stick around much longer. A phased withdrawal is the thing, like the Yanks in Vietnam.' It was one of his old jokes. Again he didn't smile. Bloody hopeless! 'Do you get the impression Hattie and Edward actually *wanted* to give this party in the first place?'

'I d-d-don't know. Maybe. I m-m-mean maybe not.' He was seriously out of it.

'Well, look, why don't we say in about an hour? I can knock up supper. Presumably you're not thinking of us going down the trat or Pizza Express or whatever.'

Guy shook his head as if those, under the circumstances, were the very worst alternatives.

'Goodness, you've really got it bad, haven't you? I'd better get home and you can come on at a decent interval, so's to give me time to scramble things together. Kitchen magic I don't think.'

This was serious, I thought. He hadn't been like it for ages, and it was weird the way he kept staring at me, when normally he never looks at anyone while talking to them. I zigzagged purposefully down the drawing room, doing my ah-ha-ha-gorgeous-to-see-you-but-must-dash bit to Sandy who I'd hardly said a word to, and El to whom I hadn't spoken all evening and who looked a bit crestfallen, since she'd wanted to introduce her new boyfriend to me for the Fudge seal of approval. So I gave him the once-over – ex-Guards wannabe actor, low lights in the perm, tan off a sunbed – whispered 'Super-shaggable!' in her ear, and was off, to use one of Poppa's favourite expressions, like a fart in a colander.

Hattie was standing by the door as if she'd been someone's mother at a dance preparing to tell me how pleased she'd been that I could make it. Only Hattie didn't look a bit pleased. What it reminded me of was that scene in *Macbeth* when we did it for exams at school, where Lady M is desperately trying to get the guests to clear out because Macbeth's behaviour has been totally cringe-inducing. I glanced towards Edward, not a bit like someone who's just seen Banquo's ghost, rather relaxed actually, then, feeling mother-hennish, I turned towards Guy, always so nice-looking when vulnerable, and caught him staring at me again. Hattie seemed as if she hadn't a clue who I was. I wondered if she might be on something. Prozac was probably stretching it a bit, but memo to ring Tricky tomorrow for the goss. Even if she was off at *Rigoletto* tonight, doing the corporate hospitality number with a smoothiechops from Paribas, she'd at least have a theory.

I drove home through the twilight wondering what on earth Guy was so desperate to unburden. He'd been seeing rather a lot of Sprue lately. In fact for the past few weeks I'd been feeling distinctly dumped for Sprue. They'd done at least three movies, including *Interview with the Vampire*, which I specially wanted to see with Guy because Brad Pitt is a serious drool for both of us, and he took her to the Poussin show at the Academy whereas I had to do it with Aunt C, who basically doesn't care for anything in art after the Middle Ages. It was odd Sprue suddenly taking up with him like this, since she'd always been a bit patronising about him before, and her family are basically anti-Jew like Catholics often are.

While I was waiting at the lights by Cadogan Square I suddenly remembered what Aunt C had said about choirs and thought what if, after all, Guy's opted to be straight. It isn't that unlikely. He's had two or three affairs with men who either turn out to be complete shits with major hang-ups, like that frightful Frenchman in Pimlico, or else dismal wimps like the sculptor (well, he said he was a sculptor) whom I used to call Clingfilm, and there's this bar in the East End he goes to where apparently they all stand around in leathers and white T-shirts thrusting out their jaws and stroking their crotches and looking desperately butch, and then get off with each other and talk about curtain materials and Delia Smith.

After a while it gets boring, I suppose. And Sprue is quite toothsome in a sort of flossy, girly, Shirley Temple, never-grown-up way, with those long brown arms she always manages to show off, and nice pert boobs, and hair done so that it looks all over the place, and that what-me-you-can't-be-serious expression in her eyes. So one could understand Guy deciding that in the end blokes weren't the thing, and it must be a terrific hit for Sprue to have an ex-gay man on her team.

I hadn't gone home by the direct route, but a bit round-the-houses so that I could nip into Europa in Draycott Avenue to get olives and anchovies for the pasta I was going to do. It's nicer than the one at the bottom of Sloane Street, which is like something in an air terminal, and I've always hated Partridges ever since Piers started that stupid argument by the check-out about baguettes. The lighting in Draycott Avenue is more subdued, and somehow I always feel it's more appropriate for this time of the evening. By now, in any case, the caliginosity factor had noticeably increased, and when I got out of the car there were little whorls of mist around the lamps, so that the street looked oddly sad and romantic under those big, gloomy trees.

Apart from a couple of German girls choosing a box of fancy biscuits as a present for somebody, I was the only person doing the loop of the supermarket, and it made me feel a bit vulnerable. Actually very vulnerable, because the bosomy Indian begum at the till gave me a motherly grin, which seriously pissed me off, so that I dropped a handful of coins on the floor and then she made it worse by exclaiming 'Ooh, deeah, deeah! T'rowing ahll your monee about!' which didn't help. Total strangers shouldn't be able to guess what you're feeling, but I knew she could.

Look, honestly, Sprue didn't worry me. After all, there's never been anything between me and Guy, and she's such a geezer – 'a trump, that Plowden girl', I remember Granny saying years ago – that she deserves him, I thought. It was just . . . well, losing Guy, not being able to bang on for hours on the phone or go into a jokey huddle at parties (like we so conspicuously hadn't tonight) or shop together or do Eurostar dashes to Le Continong or spend an evening watching crap on telly with a box of marrons glacés between us, that was what was starting to percolate. I just hated the fact that the consequences of him suddenly deciding to go straight were all mapped out so bloody precisely. When I got into the house I banged the door crossly enough for poor Mr and Mrs Martinez upstairs to have heard, and threw the carrier bag on the kitchen table. About five minutes later the bell rang and in walked Guy.

'Perfect timing,' I lied.

'G-G-God, that was ghastly, I hate every m-m-minute. All those people, like a lot of v-v-vultures picking over the carcass of c-c-conversation.'

'Love it, sweetheart, one of your best.'

'What?'

'Images.'

'Thanks, I c-c-can't think straight tonight, sorry. Everything's m-m-muddled.'

Except, apparently, what he had to tell me. Give yourself a medal for coolness, Fudge, I said to myself, gold medal with bar and oak leaves on the end of a big pink ribbon.

'Do you want that we plunge straight into the primal wilderness of supper? I thought that *sugo* I did when we were at Trasimeno was ripe for a re-think.'

'Yeh, that'd be nice.' He honestly didn't give a monkey's, I might as well have bought pot noodles. If it *was* him and Sprue he could have been a touch jollier. As it was, he looked as if he'd just come off the front line in Operation Desert Storm.

In fact – and this wasn't a trick of the light – he also looked seriously sexy, in a way I hadn't taken in before, his face long, mournful, with a kind of resigned sweetness to it, and those amazing spidery white hands, El Greco-ish altogether, an absolute Spanish monk, especially with that thinning black hair.

Frightened by what I suddenly couldn't recognise in him, I said: 'Do you want a drink first? They were a bit measly with the Lanson at Trevor Street.'

'Yeah.' He wasn't listening. 'F-F-Fudge, I've just g-g-got to tell you about this, you're the only p-p-person who . . . Oh God, it's a-a-all so fucking corny!' He kept staring at me, to the point at which I was starting to wonder what exactly he expected. The stammerometer was bad enough, but now I'd begun to get fidgety too.

'Come into the kitch,' I said, 'and talk to me while I'm throwing the spag. Actually it's fettucine, but same difference.'

We migrated. Halfway along the corridor, Guy put out a clumsy hand and held me for a moment by the arm.

'You're t-t-tremendously important to me in ways I can't . . .' Then he burst out laughing, a pained, half-hysterical snort. 'I can't f-f-finish my s-s-sentences tonight.'

I made my brave-little-girl smile. The germ of a truly weird idea had planted itself in my mind. What if? God, no, it couldn't be, but the trouble is you never know with Guy. By now mega embarrassed and starting to feel magnanimously sorry for old Sprue, whom I'd sort of sussed out wasn't the thing after all, I began clattering ferociously among the cupboards, turning round only to say breezily: 'Look, do sit down, I'm not going to use the whole table, you know. Do you want Scotch?'

'N-n-no, I'd rather have gin. Look, w-w-what I'm going to tell you may be a b-b-bit of a shock . . .'

'I shouldn't imagine it's anything more shocking than what you've told me in the past,' said I, lying strenuously and compounding it by asking: 'Do you want me to sit and listen, or do you mind if I potter about while you talk?'

'No, please p-p-potter. I can t-t-trust you to listen.'

Do I want this, I thought, do I seriously want Guy to do what he's now going to, and tell me that he's fallen in love with me and wants me to make an honest man of him and that he's fed up with standing about in bars and taking home dreary boys called Ricky and Darrens, who wear white Calvin Klein underpants and sell water-filters and bathroom tiles in John Lewis's basement? I suppose I should have been flattened, but I wasn't, simply because of details like this, the sort that make us both hoot every time Guy describes them to me. I don't mind being an alternative, it's just that I didn't want to be an alternative to Darren. Guy was silent all of a sudden, and I heard him taking some of those deep breaths his speech therapist recommended when things got out of control.

'Well, go on,' I heard myself say, grotesquely unsympathetic as I yanked out the cheese-grater from the drawer by the sink. He said nothing, just sat there ventilating, his hands on the table, staring into the gloom beyond the open window. Remembering his drink, I hurriedly got out the gin and a glass. The whole situation had become simply bloody, and threatened to get still bloodier when he started to utter again.

'I know you'll think it's c-c-crazy, but this . . . Oh, it's . . .'

Unbearable, I could have said, only something blessedly stopped me. Usually I'm rather good at leading people on towards the moment when they offload their intimate confessions, but right now I felt strangely disinclined. The only thing I could think of doing was to open the fridge door and stare hard at what lay inside, purely so as to keep my back turned to Guy while he talked. Or tried to.

'I-I-It's about E-E-Edward, Edward Martindale. We've been s-s-seeing each other. In the evenings, mostly, after he goes to the g-g-gym. Hattie thinks he's w-w-working late, but he isn't. He comes to see me. It's o-o-on his way home, after all.'

That sounded oddly like an excuse, and in any case Graham Terrace is hardly on a direct route from Finsbury Avenue to

Trevor Street. This, of course, was not the point. I was supposed to react, to say something like 'Edward! How long has this been going on?' All I did instead was squat down beside the fridge, pretending to hunt for the tonic, obviously there in front of me, next to the jar of mayonnaise and the olive paste, so yummy on cream crackers, and the remains of last night's salad. Absurdly I began pulling everything out and putting it on the floor. Guy must have guessed something of what I felt, though certainly not all, but he blundered on, fatally encouraged by my silence.

'I-I-It just happened one evening, when he t-t-turned up on the d-d-doorstep and said he thought he'd drop by on the o-o-offchance I was in.'

And you bloody were, I thought, not needing Guy to tell me how nice Edward looked in his head-to-toe Armani with the ash-blond angel curls tumbling around his forehead, and how they'd got at the vodka and watched *Top Gun*, which just happened to be on telly that evening, and grew ever so altogether in the process. I opened the freezer and noisily plonked a packet of kippers on top of the tiramisu ice cream.

So one thing led to another, evidently. The burning question appeared to be whether Edward had done it with any other men before Guy, presumably so that Guy could feel a bit safer about being his . . . Well it's what the French call *cinq à sept*, isn't it? Guy's always said that if ever he becomes a woman in his next life, this is what he'll opt for, some mega chic existence as a middle-aged *b.c.b.g.* parisienne in rue de l'Université or rue de Lille, getting it regularly from a dashing Eurocrat who turns up out of the twilight quoting Baudelaire before going home to sweet Catholic wifey in the *seizième*.

But oh no, apart from getting the hots for someone at Sherborne and casting a few lingering glances in the direction of the hunkier numbers at the gym, Edward was officially straight until that evening. And any hopes Guy might have had regarding a cosy *cinq à sept* arrangement, with Edward bombing round after a day's wheeler-dealing to get his rocks off in that preposterous French bed Sandy helped Guy to buy, bless her, off the bottom of the Fulham Road were dashed after a few sessions.

'What, he couldn't hack it?' I concluded, as if trying to tie everything up breezily. Long before this I'd finally turned round and administered the gin shot, having generally run out of things to do in the fridge and got bored with being embarrassed. He sat there at the table, his fingers curling round the glass like wisteria.

'N-N-No, worse than that.'

'You don't fancy him any more.' I didn't mean that to sound too hopeful.

'For C-C-Christ's sake, how not? You should see him with his c-c-clothes off.'

'Yeah, well, I've seen him in a swimming costume and his bum's to die for. So?'

Guy took a demure sip of his gin, and gave a funny little secret smile, the sort that for a split second always makes him look fearfully old and knowing, though he's only twenty-eight.

'Fudge, Edward's . . . he's f-f-fallen in love with me.'

'Oh shit.'

The medal I now awarded myself was the DSO, the DS standing for Desperately Sophisticated. We sat there for an hour pulling the whole thing to and fro like something out of *Just Seventeen* or that woman in the *Sun* who can't spell her name properly. In fact we pulled it so many ways it got like bloody origami. After a couple more gins Guy decided he wasn't hungry any more, so I made us a sandwich instead with the olive paste, and we tried without any success whatever to decide what he should do about Edward, hyper-bonkable but evidently not heartbreak material.

Then at about half past eleven Guy announced he was going home. Getting up and stretching, he gave a little snort of laughter and said: 'Now is the way c-c-clear, now is the m-m-meaning plain, I don't think. C-C-Caliginous just ain't in it.'

Then, when I'd seen him to the door and he was going down the steps, he turned and whispered: 'You know, F-F-Fudge, he may have a gorgeous b-b–bum, but when it comes to post-coital ch-ch-chat he's a total yawn.'

I went back into the kitchen and sat down for a moment at the table, the white and yellow Europa bag still unemptied in front of me, looking as if it had crashed out there from sheer exhaustion. The thing to do at this point would have been for me to have a little cry, sitting there on my own, just having not been proposed to by someone who for at least twenty minutes I'd allowed myself to imagine was secretly in love with me. Goodness, hadn't I done brilliantly, given how totally gobsmacked I was by the whole thing, and conscious, what's more, of having been an utter prat for not guessing. Not Darren, not Ricky, or even Sprue or me, but Edward. But I didn't feel at all like having a weep. After a while, getting up and opening the door on to the terrace, I wandered out into the garden. The night was amazingly warm for early summer in London, and there was this incredible stillness everywhere, as though that funny mist I'd noticed earlier round the street lamps was really cotton wool muffling the sounds of the cars or the people in the neighbouring houses. The Iranians next door had their lights on and so did Mr and Mrs Martinez. I wondered if they'd heard what Guy said as he left. Or what they'd think if they saw me drifting about in my Nicole Farhi, alone in the dark garden.

Everything all of a sudden felt nice again, specially the fact that we hadn't sorted anything out and so in a sense I'd been useless. It meant we'd go on much as we had before, with Guy telling me the funnier bits about sex as he always does, while the whole thing got more and more serious on Edward's part, which must mean that in the end Guy would back off completely. The thought of Edward talking solemnly about making a commitment was toe-curling for both of us.

And we'd hardly mentioned Hattie, except in a general what-if-she-finds-out kind of way. Standing there in the garden with the smell coming off the camphor bush in the corner and something equally delicious from next door's lilac, I felt distantly sorry for her. Of course, it all ought to have seemed more of a mess, yet somehow it didn't, just because I hadn't lost Guy, I suppose, which sounds awful, but you know what I mean. Then I thought of Trevor Street and the shiny door-knocker and that Gothick pattern along the wallpaper in the hall and those fat cushions in the drawing room which look as if someone's been at them with a bicycle pump and the fluffy Victorian sketches in black frames and that Persian rug Edward's always fussing about and everything utterly hunky-dory under the light of those clean, clean windows. And I thought of Edward in the corner, beautiful and boring and lusting after Guy. Then I remembered how sour Hattie looked at the party, her eyes suspecting but not knowing. What's really sad – it just came to me as I stood there in the garden – is that we've never ever given her a nickname.

The Smile of the Diva

'The last time I came here,' I said, 'they were disgustingly rude, in that professional way the French have of being totally foul and expecting you to sit up and beg for more. Maybe it's because they're in England and they feel they have to put on a show. Or just because they're frightened of being abroad.

'Anyway, they were vile. I was with Polly, when she was still at Trubshaw Goldsticker, just before she got the push. She was particularly vulnerable that evening, as though she knew it was coming. She was even wearing a hat, something I'd never seen her do before, an enormous thing like a ship, with the brim curved up at one end in a kind of transom effect.

'I thought it was this hat the waiters didn't like, but maybe it was just the sight of the pair of us together. We sat in the window talking for ages, while they mooched about smoking up and down the room and spreading themselves over the chairs. After about half an hour Polly got impatient and stopped one of them as he was coming out of the kitchen. He peered at her under the hat and said, with a satirical force you wouldn't have thought it possible to give the two words: "Vous désirez?"

'Polly simply said: "We'd like some food." He shrugged and went back into the kitchen, and we heard him exclaim: "Ces gens! Ils veulent du *food*, euh?"

'It must have been another fifteen minutes before they brought us a menu. And then when we ordered the wine, the waiter couldn't resist scoring a completely unjustifiable point off Polly. She knew they had a Burgundy she was particularly fond of called Rully, and when she asked for it, the smart-arsed sod deliberately mispronounced it as Rouilly so as to make her think she'd got it wrong. After that she practically collapsed. She and the hat.'

You smiled, less out of compassion for Polly than towards me for my over-strenuous elaboration of the story. I was trying to impress you and you'd caught me in the act. It was something you knew all about because, in the past, you'd done it so often yourself. At university, I remember, you were somebody whose name one grew sick of the sound of precisely for not being one's own; somebody who, by disseminating at least four different versions of his life story, all nineteen years of it, had achieved just the correct measure of notoriety to get him asked to parties to see if he could come up with another, a boy whose sexuality was carefully arranged to present a number of different possibilities, like one of those all-weather tennis courts which used to be advertised by a firm called En Tout Cas. People liked the hints of collusion suggested by your lean jaws, your big, consequential teeth, your leonine black hair and large ears. Small ears on a man are so unsexy. Besides which it was said that you could play Scriabin sonatas and went seriously to the gym.

No doubt it was easy to imagine you combining the two, rippling up and down the Bechstein in stretch leisurewear, endowed with a sanitized eroticism *à la* Calvin Klein. Some of us, however, prefer implausibility. In spite of what people say, genuineness is always less attractive than the implications of pretence. I had a feeling that you knew this as you sat there talking in your soft, furtively intense voice which I didn't want to believe was only a variant on the sort of stop you pulled out when lunching clients. Yet there was also something of pure instinct in the assumption you seemed to make that I'd find total integrity altogether banal – quite right of course as a general rule, but wrong, as it happened, just then.

Did you notice the way I kept looking at your hands? I'm always doing it, for the simple reason that my own are so completely nondescript, always staring at other people's big, thick fingers and wondering why on earth mine, with their ridiculous lumpy nails and ugly gatherings of skin just below the whites, haven't got anything like the same character and distinctiveness. At the bottom of the left-hand index, where it meets the fist, there's a scar, almost invisible now, made when I cut myself on the tin box containing the ink pad of a child's printing set given to me as a present on my fourth birthday. That's the sole claim to individuality presented by either of my hands, and you can hardly see it anyway.

I wanted yours to be my hands. The little feints at greater intimacy you kept making, slithering one or another of them towards me across the table cloth, rearranging your glasses of wine and water so as to clear a runway for your extended fingers, using them as punctuators and adornments of your enchantingly murmured discourse, were all, had you known it, utterly pointless. Even if you weren't that old – twenty-nine by my computation, though, on one or two recent occasions when I'd seen you, looking decidedly thirty-fivish – you'd lived long enough to have become convinced that most people wanted you, for whatever purpose. At first it seemed odd to me, in trying to recover the essence of that lunch at La Marjolaine, that I couldn't summon up a recollection of anything like desire. Now I realise – or rather, I acknowledge, because the realisation was always there – that if you'd dropped the pantomime and frankly offered me yourself raw to the touch, I'd have asked instead for your identity, for the power to be you, to be able to twist those thick, serious hands of yours on to the ends of my arms like Hoover attachments and abseil nonchalantly across spread chords and consecutive ninths.

Somebody else, I was sure, had understood this. As the

ribbon of our talk wound on, orchestrated with the waiter's interventions of mange-tout and potatoes, a second bottle of mineral water and a knife to replace the one I'd tremulously dropped on the floor at a moment when your teeth assumed a particularly unsettling air of sincerity, I began to notice, at first simply for want of somewhere else to look, the woman seated at the next table. I'm hopeless, anyway, at eye contact. Apparently it's something you learn when joining the Foreign Legion, the unflinching stare, a sort of ocular arm-wrestling which you must be calculated absolutely to win. Of course I can think of more immediately alluring reasons for becoming a legionnaire, but just acquiring that stare seems to me the most abundantly useful. As it is, I inspire an immediate mistrust in others by not looking directly at them. You can imagine – you particularly – what it's like for me on the Continent, where hooking yourself instantly on to someone else's gaze is almost an article of religion. It sounds silly, I know, but the reason I can't bring myself to do it is because I'm frightened people will think I'm falling in love with them.

Isn't that the craziest thing you ever heard? A species of egoism really, the belief that my mythic glance, a gorgon, a basilisk and a Raphael Madonna rolled into one, wields too titanic a potency for me not to have some compassion on those towards whom I turn it. So instead of looking at you, I stared, however sheepishly at first, in the direction of the woman so comfortably arranged against the steep red velvet ribbing of the banquette, whose slightly tilted mirror above reflected the waves of her ash-blonde hair and the little starts and quivers made by her green earrings and the pink scarf around her throat as she nodded her head and laughed to her companion across the table.

The awful thing is that for the purposes of this story I really ought to have tried to remember what he looked like, yet, you know, honestly I can't, except that he was bald and squat and round-shouldered and wore a light-grey suit. If he had any sort of definable air, it was that of being condemned for ever to be thought of in terms of an escort, a walker, the insignificant other whose flavourless exchanges of conversation must always have made her more interested in sampling the gamier mutualities of the adjacent tables.

Silly then she kept glancing towards us as he spoke, and even when having to respond with something more than a nod or an 'aha' of polite concordance, she kept an eye, as it were, on our shared animation, watched your big, convincing hands with what seemed almost like my own fascination as they continually shuffled to and from the food on your plate, the glass, the token vase of pinks or the mineral water bottle, as if making successive versions of a text in order to impose on it the particular reading which should suit your purposes. Because you've never told me, have you, what you wanted, and I'm far too stupid not to need the kind of first-base ABC enlightenment which, by its very simplicity, is always impossible to ask for directly.

But the woman knew, or so I started to assume whennow and then my eyes, however hard they tried not to, came to meet hers, so limped with what looked like indulgence and sympathy that I couldn't decide whether I resented such intrusive compassion or whether instead I wanted nakedly to demand her help with my mounting confusions. We'd started, hadn't we, to talk about music, and you were telling me how, just like poor Polly in her *Fighting Téméraire* of a hat, advertising was only something you did as a job and that you'd wanted, goodness how you'd wanted, to be a serious musician and how you envied me being able to compose and create and communicate – the impacted clichés threatened to undermine your air of coming clean, but for once I gave you the benefit of the doubt. Did I like Rachmaninov? You were mad for him yourself. In fact, Russian music, you could honestly declare, was your poison. Proust or somebody, wasn't it, said music was the brandy of the damned. Shaw actually, I muttered with relentless pedantry, thinking if you're going to try and impress me this way, get it right for Christ's sake, even if this wasn't the way in which I wanted to be impressed.

And all the time I wondered why are you doing this, talking about the Prokofiev violin concertos and some Tchaikovsky pieces, 'The Seasons', a friend had just given you, sketches, you said, deceptively simple but in reality a test of a decent pianist, and these two symphonies by a composer called Kalinnikov you'd discovered quite by chance in Tower Records, why are you trying to make me think you're dissatisfied – since enthusiasm, perversely considered, is a form of dissatisfaction – when actually I know you're not, when your life, as I've pieced it together, is a system of satiating distinct appetites with the assistance of money earned from work you claim disgusts you?

while I listened, fine-tuning the degree of attentiveness I could sense you plausibly begging for, and feeling perhaps (though again I can't recall this exactly) some sympathy for the walker in the grey suit filling the chair next to mine, I noticed a still more intense alertness in the face of the woman opposite. The waiter came to take their order for pudding, and as he stood over them, his black-trousered arse insufficient yet irksomely blocking my view, she actually turned her head and smiled at me, a smile, I should have said at that moment, of total complicity, roguish, conspiratorial, but also with a faint weariness to it, as if what she knew, or thought she knew, to be happening between us were something she had watched in this situation a thousand times before. 'I could tell you,' said the smile, a temporary concession to amusement in features which otherwise retained a certain heavy-lidded, potentially dramatic sombreness, '(I could tell you what will happen next, I could tell you what not to do, what words or gestures to avoid, yet I could also tell you that you wouldn't listen, and that however much you believed me, you'd get everything catastrophically wrong and make the most dismal mess of it. So what on earth's the use?'

Turning, the waiter started to move away, but the smile

stayed there in the woman's face, in a suspension which looked as if it was calling on me to respond. Of course you hadn't noticed any of this, and said something like 'Do you think I should?' to which I had to answer instead, and try to look at you, at that extraordinary innocent you seemed all of a sudden to have become, the tips of your large ears growing rather red, your black mane flung back from your forehead as a guarantee of just how candid you were prepared to be with me – which of course was nothing of the sort – and your brown eyes a child's demanding absolute trust.

Yet also a liar's. People so habitually dishonest as you are betray themselves not necessarily because we wonder what monstrous fibs and mythomaniacal taradiddles they will perpetrate next, but sometimes simply by their absurd willingness to believe in us. The more lies they tell, the less proof they are against our lying, and it's for this we despise them often far more than for their inability to tell the truth. The woman, I was certain, understood this. By now she was invested with positively sybilline powers of intuition. The little wisp of steam rising from the coffee in front of her might have been that of some sacrificial offering in a consecrated vessel. A hint of that intuitive smile still waited around the corners of her mouth, as though she were enjoying, precisely for being able to discern it so clearly, your renewed pantomime of seduction. Want me, your hands said, brushing against mine with a casualness quite desperate in its calculation, want me, said the knots in the corners of your nutcracker jaws and the shoulders sheer as parapets in the ascetic architectural diagram of your black suit. The shading of that smile told me what I wanted to say and couldn't, about what I'd felt earlier, about telling you not to bother, even though I knew you couldn't help it, that it was what you did with everyone, a sort of automatic pilot, a mode into which you entered because the real thing was so much more difficult to cope with. She knew, did the woman at the next table, how much of you I longed to dismantle, carrying off thereafter those relevant pieces which should take the place of everything in my own physicality – nearly all of it indeed – I'd ever found embarrassing or insubstantial.

Even the waiter, a leggy, cadaverous Berber, with teeth even bigger than yours, wasn't safe. The way you asked for the bill with you head on one side and an ear-to-ear, boyish, oh-God-I-know-it's-such-a-bore-but-could-we-please   grin, anyone would have fancied you were expecting him to scribble his phone number on the back. Fubsy Mr Other at the next table had already paid theirs. *She* evidently wasn't the sort who dealt with money, and I rather liked that. Sybils, in my experience, don't flourish wads or carry plastic. They got up to leave, and while you were having a last ogle with Larbi from Ouarzazate or wherever (that sort, by the way – or course you knew but it didn't stop you – sends remittances *outre-Manche* to wife and kids in some grim towerblock in Gennevillers or Asnières) I turned round to watch the woman putting on her coat, or having it put on for her. There was a little good-mannered banter in French with *le patron*, his surliness implausibly substituted by servility, and then, as he began almost bowing her into the street (the faceless one picked up an ort or two of this unaccustomed charm simply for following her towards the door), she looked back, to smile once more in my direction. It was what somebody in an old play refers to as 'a demure travel of regard', daring me again to respond. Daring isn't something I'm good at. When we made to leave, the mysterious good humour which appeared to have settled on the staff, a result of them having fawned on the tall blonde woman as they robed her in her charcoal-grey coat like acolytes draping a cope round the shoulders of a bishop, bestowed some of its aura absent-mindedly on us.

'Maybe you know who that was,' said the most low-life of the waiters, the one who, I now recalled, had been so hard on poor Polly about the wine, with a number-one crop and a cold sore on his inferior lip. Silly us, we hadn't a clue, so indulgently he pronounced the name of a tremendously celebrated American diva currently figuring at Covent Garden. 'She always comes here,' said the low-life, 'she likes that we know who she is.'

Bet she does, I thought, bet she's just gagging for everyone to come up and ask her to sign last night's programme and tell her how brilliantly she hit that top B flat in 'Regnava nel silenzio', and how much they loved her Norma at the Bastille, and was it true she as going to do Leonora at the Met next year? In that moment I hard the temple doors clatter open. The chafing-dish with its newly scattered incense fell to the floor, the garlands around the altar withered abruptly, the tripod keeled over and my pythoness was revealed merely as that most trifling of existential units, an entertainer, wreathed with nothing more solid than the hooha of gallery adulation and her own vulgar insecurities. She had cheated me then, with the soft, inclusive warmth of her smile into which I'd read such volumes of patient comprehension, when all the time it wasn't that in the least. There's a northern word we use in my family, 'nesh', which means raw, vulnerable or not proof against even the slightest contrariness offered by ordinary events. My peculiar neshness I'd thought she could understand, just as I supposed that with no particular difficulty she'd gauged the sort of hustler you were trying to be. Not even trying, if it came to that.

As it was, she hadn't even guessed a thing, hadn't even especially wanted to know. People like that are incurious about anything except the degree to which the public is prepared to go in expressing love and fidelity towards them. The diva's smile had been waiting, not on my confession, but on my recognition, on some wretchedly ordinary instant in which I was expected to exclaim: 'Excuse me, but aren't you . . .' or 'Golly gee, Miss——, I really loved your *portamento* in the Mad Scene the other night.' My self-consciousness is valuable, a commodity I don't like to waste, and she had angered me by trifling with it. Recalled, the smile felt like a door one pulls, finds won't budge, pushes too hard and ends up falling flat on the other side of it.

In the end it was your fault. God knows how, but it was. Opening the car door, you announced you were off to the gym, where, I sardonically pictured some poor guy getting a hard-on in the shower while you soaped yourself lovingly with your own brand of self-consciousness. 'Magic to know things are doing so well,' you said, giving my hand such a strong tug that your own nearly came off. 'Call me,' you said, and for a second it sounded as if you really thought I would.

It's Never You

Dotted with plain trees and scruffy-looking hawthorns, its rough lawn covered by a light occupational layer of drink cans, cigarette packets and the exhausted apparatus of last night's cruising, the triangular patch of woodland marking the southwestern end of Clapham Common is a haunt, on summer days, of gay men. They settle on the grass with nonchalant assurance, like birds, and the dog-led women and haphazard children treading the paths among the coppices could be forgiven for thinking that at the sound of a handclap these bodies, burnished and hairless amid each towelled encampment carefully picketed by a Walkman, a rucksack, a pair of caterpillar boots and a half-litre bottle of mineral water, might flutter effortlessly into the air to perch in the branches before resuming their studied balance of composure with enticement.

None of them was more critical that afternoon than Cal and Tom, and their asperity was perhaps the sharper because Matt had made them laugh as he always did with his neat little characterisations of those scattered across the newly shaven clearing. More than a hint or two of transgression in his white, eel-thin body, razored head and near nakedness emphasised rather than absolved by a pair of exiguous navy shorts meant that in a slightly guarded way both boys found him attractive. You never actually encountered Matt or saw him coming. In the club, in the street, he showed and disappeared with equal abruptness, just as he had done now, grinning pertly from the shadow of a tree.

'Mmm, yeah, tasty,' he muttered, 'but probably got an attitude problem. Italian, you can tell from the size of his packet. And that cross way he looks at everyone, as if it's their fault he's bored. They're always bored, Italians. Boring an Italian's like pissing in the sea, so fucking easy you wonder why you bother.'

The others sniggered. Matt pulled a cigarette from the pack inside his sock and lit it.

'Tell us about those two over there by the bench,' said Tom.

'Well, the tan's probably genuine, Ibiza if they got lucky, a few away-days at Brighton if they didn't. They microwave the low-calorie stuff they buy at the Balham Safeway and eat it with tomato salad and a Kiwis Surprise for afters. And they tiff about things like who gets to choose the new duvet cover before they've even had time to think what colour it's going to be.'

He paused to allow their collective scrutiny to wheel freely among the sunbathers, one licking a thoughtful finger over a copy of *Hello*, another swaying ditsily to the cicada-scratch of his Walkman, and three in the shade of a straggling thorn bush methodically engaged in the serious business of protective anointment. After a while Cal's eye fixed with some interest on the awkward-looking figure questing an inconspicuous space in the long grass by the path leading down towards the bandstand. Matt, seeing him at the same moment, laughed indulgently.

'Now that, Cal sweetheart, in case you didn't know, is a biddy.'

'A what?'

'A biddy if ever I saw one: shorts are a dead giveaway and the hair he can't do anything with, and that Tupperware sandwich box he's got. Bet his mum gave it him before he came to live in London. Like Dick Whittington or something, all he wants is the cat. "Now, our Nigel", she said as she stood at the cottage door with the honeysuckle round it, "don't you let those nasty men get after you, and mind you keep your sausage roll inside a bit of Tupperware." Jesus, it's too much, per-lease!'

Matt rolled over on his back, pedalling his DM'd feet in the air in helpless delight at the precision of his hypothesis.

'What's a biddy anyway?' asked Tom.

'You know, a gay nerd. He'll do things like walking the Pennine Way or going birdwatching in the Hebrides instead of getting his end away in Miami Beach. And he'll have this humungous collection of classical CDs he wipes with a special cloth before he puts them in the stereo. And he'll make slides of all his holidays and rabbit on about frigging shutter-speeds and apertures. It's the only kind of aperture that sort knows anything about.'

Springing acrobatically to his feet and tugging up the back of his shorts, Matt eyed both boys quizzically for a moment as if preparing them for the same devastating vignette.

'Do you know what?' Again he snorted with laughter. 'Biddies never sleep naked. They're worried their bollocks'll drop off during the night and they won't be able to find them next morning when they make the bed.' And they could just hear him hiss, as he winced back among the trees: 'With hospital corners!'

If Tom and Cal experienced a faint twinge of relief at watching Matt disappear, it was because they envied him. Or thought they did at least. True, the memory of their single visit to the squat off Coldharbour Lane where he dwelt alongside an indeterminate presence of ambulant nose-pierced girls, still made them shudder. There was no heating to speak of, fragments chipped from the plaster with its archaeology of floral wallpapers disclosed eloquent gashes of naked brickwork, and sedulously unshaded lightbulbs hung from the woodchip ceilings. Opening the fridge in a misguided access of curiosity, Tom had found it empty save for a flask of popper and a half-consumed packet of cheese slices. Their shared recollection battened delightedly on the *Schadenfreude* in such details, yet something out of this impatient abnegation of comfort gave them a sense of nagging insufficiency regarding their own sincere attempts at cultivating the appropriate hardness.

For one thing, they lived in Wandsworth. It was only just Wandsworth, the demarcation apparently running down the middle of the street, but a surrounding *embourgeoisement*, in the shape of builders' skips, freshly laid gravel in the driveways and the brashness of new door-knockers, was beginning to make them uneasily aware that this sort of thing would never have menaced them had they only opted for the dustbowl of Clapham North or the frowzier eastern skirts of Kennington. Even the guy recently installed in the maisonette downstairs, promising initially when they'd seen him taking care of a partner at Dirty Dishes whose E had come up too quickly, turned out to keep a spaniel and went to work in what looked suspiciously like Next suiting.

Neither Cal nor Tom would have been seen dead in a Next suit, and judged a dog second only to a cat in the naffness scale. They knew people, of course, who lived like this, queens who gave each other tips about cushion covers, visited garden centres and grew florid on the theme of getting the right mix for the primrose emulsion which should bring the spare bedroom walls up a treat. Such anxieties served by antithesis to heighten their own as to living on the frontier of an engulfing cosiness, so that minimalism came to seem the only answer. Each evening they returned to the integrity of a reverberative emptiness, in which their shared existence was defined by assorted negatives, by the things a painstaking scrutiny of available options had enabled them providently not to buy, the places a single visit counselled them to avoid, and all those auguries which croaked a warning of the predictable or the commonplace.

Wandsworth, as it happened was hardly their fault, any

more than the bottle-green Fiat Punto they drove. The flat was rented at a generous discount from Cal's brother-in-law, while the car had been dropped on them, as it were, via the casual benevolence of a youthful widowed aunt of Tom's who ran a garage in Caterham and thought a gay nephew was something agreeably raffish, a nice conversation-stopper for the other girls at hen nights over the third or fourth Malibu, as long, mind, as he didn't come visiting with Cal too often. At least it was a Punto and not a Polo or, worst of all, some poxy little Micra with a family in the back. They were careful not to drive it to the Wimbledon Ikea or to be seen together loading the boot with bags from the Clapham Junction Iceland. Unpolluted by domesticity, the vehicle had simply to be the means whereby they were able to arrive with minimum fuss at Trade around two in the morning after an unimproving couple of hours getting vapourised amid the gropers or Pleasuredrome, or to do the Anvil without having to stand about in that embarrassing post-party queue for minicabs. Otherwise they courted the aleatoric delights of bus and Underground, scenting a keener distillation of urbanism in the Northern Line's casual promiscuities or in the vistas disclosed from the top of a 137 bucking and snorting across Chelsea Bridge.

Thus too you risked encounters. Obsessive fidelity was never an issue with either of them. Tom might observe Cal nonchalantly up-ending some other guy over the pool table on Monday nights at Substation, or himself be glanced at as the centrepiece of tantric entanglements within a steam cloud, but this was scarcely solid ground for divorce. In the *Sunday Times*, to which somewhat shamefacedly they'd returned after a profitless flirtation with a more liberal rival, a detail in an article on Edward VII and Queen Alexandra had much amused them: the consort's remark, in the presence of Mrs Keppel as both women stood by the dead king's bedside, that 'he was my naughty little man but he always came home to me'. To Cal, who came home later than Tom from work, there was infinite reassurance in finding him there on the sofa scanning the pages of *Attitude* or *Wallpaper* with that frown of earnest concentration only Conran Shop coathangers or a pair of Patrick Cox wannabes could seriously evoke. As for Tom, it was impossible to imagine anyone else sharing the peculiar intensity of his impatience with those whose absence of coolness – his version of it, at any rate – made them sloppy or deliberately negligent of the issues which ineluctably rated.

On this, indeed, Cal was still more draconian than his lover. Compounding a first name out of his three initials was simply another means of defining himself through essentials, like the bleached floorboards of their bedroom or the beech-wood cubes which held the white bathtowels from Muji. He never told anyone what he was really called, and mostly they knew better than to ask. A species of visionary restlessness in him, as if always thinking about where both of them might shift next so as to remain beyond the reach of mere good taste, sometimes almost frightened Tom, alerting him to the possibility that he himself might be capable in Cal's eyes of those very same solecisms of selection and adornment he was so quick to condemn in others. To be thrown aside for any guy more blatantly attractive wasn't something Tom felt he needed specially to fear, but to be chucked for failing at the fences of style presented the ultimate nightmare of mortifying rejection.

Given sombrely to imagining this from time to time, he'd consider that perhaps the strongest assurance of not getting left behind by his lover derived paradoxically from the fact that for long periods during the week the pair of them hardly saw one another. While Tom went to work in a television studio in Golden Square, Cal set out for a restaurant off Pont Street where, dressed in a grey T-shirt and black jeans, advantageous to the lines of his body yet still emphatically anonymous, he glossed the men's deliberate textual vague-nesses, took care not to overfill the slender-stemmed goblets with Beringer Fumé Blanc and maintained a chaste, sometimes consciously teasing detachment from the punters over their crab cakes and celeriac. Some of them were famous, and those who weren't diffused the sort of non-specific glamour whose aura afforded Cal something like job satisfaction, but he knew better than to try grappling them to him with awestruck recognition or congratulations. Not acknowledging them as anything more than movable elements among the slate-topped tables to which he carried Ferrarelle and rocket salad brought a lonely delight which hugged him yet as he jumped from the bus at the corner of Cedars Road and walked the last stretch home through the crisp night. Letting himself into the flat and finding it still there, its planes of pale colour, carefully scooped pools of shadow and deliberate rhetorical spaces resisting brashness or inattentive suggestions of cosiness, he fancied he could discern who he was.

One day, of course – there had to be the 'of course' – he and Tom would go and live in New York. How this might happen wasn't yet clear, not did they dare to sift through the relevant practicalities, but Manhattan, hints of whose sophistication they'd absorbed for a single delirious October week as the guests of a designer breathlessly courted one night at The Hoist during the kind of interstitial moment which the Germans call 'an art pause', now presented them with a flawlessly etched grid of desires awaiting ultimate fulfilment. London, meanwhile, needed negotiating in all its tiresome obliquity, yet they'd always known how to handle that. If at times their friends seemed insufficient to the challenges they posed, if Kevin and Mark's new blinds looked too flagrantly Peter Jones, if Jason and Steve served seared tuna with iceberg lettuce instead of watercress, and if Gianluca wasn't nearly Milanese enough in his penchant for cheap cardigans, Tom and Cal could be magnanimous, because they understood how tough was even the mere embarkation on those myriad preliminary soundings and accountings which should ensure that such elements were slid properly into place.

Such awareness, with all its appropriate shadings of dread, meant that for much of the time the pair were careful not to operate too closely as an item and sometimes went to extraordinary lengths to sustain this illusion of autonomy. Rather than going together to Fist, for instance, they'd arrange that Tom would take the car while Cal, who enjoyed biking more, pedalled the length of Acre Lane, however fully accoutred in leathers, to meet his lover by chance, as it were, in the subterranean gloom. It was an article of faith, what was more, that they should never be seen supermarket shopping side by side, even if seeming casually to happen on the same store at a given instant. The game they played, here as elsewhere, was with others' expectations, but as always it was Cal rather than Tom who drew up the rules and made sure of the anticipatory manoeuvres.

A perfect excuse for such independence offered itself some days after their encounter with Matt on the Common. A Saturday when both were free, it was spoiled for Tom by a call the previous evening demanding his attendance at the studio tomorrow.

'Fuck it!' He banged down the telephone and pounded the back of the chair with his fists. 'I wanted to go and look for some new blades.'

'There's nothing that says you can't,' said Cal, defusing the other's annoyance with his tranquil grey stare. 'They're not going to keep you there all day.'

'Yeah, but I don't know that, do I? There's this bit of film they got wrong, and we could be like hours checking it through. What are you going to do, anyway?'

'Go to Brighton and get some sun if it's fine like today.'

'Oh yeah, while I'm shut up in the studio, jammy bastard. Do you want the car?'

'No, I'll take the bike on the train.' Cal flashed a satanic grin. 'And there's some of that couscous salad left if you get hungry and I'm not home.'

'Fuck off!'

Rather as Tom feared, the weather next morning was of a kind which made stewing in a Soho basement the last thing he'd ever have chosen to do on a Saturday. Cal, padding about in his 2Xist while unhurriedly fixing himself a double espresso, saw him to the door, then sat down for a moment before the opened kitchen window with his coffee. The smell of gardens and earth and warm leaves, vague but enticing, was borne into the house on the little gusts of air that brushed like hands against his skin. As the day began plotting itself in his mind while he showered, pulled on his cycling trunks and tugged up the laces on his boots, some inchoate impulse of perversity, connected partly with where at this moment he could imagine himself want to be, and much more obscurely with the figure of Matt, mocking and tattooed, recalled from yesterday, began to take possession of him. He hadn't lied to Tom at the moment he told him he was going to Brighton. In his rucksack were a bathing towel, the printed cotton beach sheet a friend had brought them from Italy, a tube of Vichy Laqit Solaire, a small Volvic bottle and his Walkman with the relevant tapes of 'Wave Speech', 'Guido the Killer Pimp' and 'Calm Down', all as pledges of his good faith. Yet as the train pulled southwards along the edge of Tooting Common, already looking dry-mouthed and sluttish under the rising heat, and into Streatham, kicking piss-elegant heels against the trackside sycamores, Cal acknowledged this new imperative, however dimly, as meaning he'd never make it.

The sign for which he was waiting came at a station somewhere beyond Horsham where the train refused to budge. There was a crackle on the public address system, and then the conductor came down the carriage saying 'Sorry, ladies and gents, I'm afraid we're going to have to wait up a bit because there's a signal failed outside Hassocks. Shouldn't be long though.' For a moment Cal sat back nervelessly, smelling the sun on the blue moquette and quizzing the surrounding passengers from behind the safety of his Cutler & Gross. A woman in a black sleeveless T-shirt played impatiently with the ends of her hair, while another, older and more resigned to such misadventures, began leafing resolutely through *Prima*, licking a finger as she did so with a fastidiousness contradicted by the action itself. On one of the seats beyond, a plump, bespectacled boy, sweating through his white shirt, took an energy bar out of a little green holdall and started to munch it between scanning something called *International Coin Collector* and making notes in the back of a pocket diary. Cal remembered Matt's anatomising of a biddy and smiled to himself at wondering what the boy wore in bed.

Almost certainly pyjamas. Getting up, he wandered down the train till he came to the luggage van where he'd put his bike. Pulling a window down, he peered out at the empty station. Then, as if it had been the most natural reaction in the world, he opened the door, unlocked the bike and sprang down with it on to the platform. Pausing only to check the timetable for afternoon trains – even at so momentous an instant his calculating instincts never deserted him – he swung a leg over the crossbar, got himself comfortable in the saddle and pushed off among the nondescript white railway cottages on to the main road out of the town.

It thrilled Cal profoundly that he had never done anything of this sort before, yet when afterwards he contemplated the peculiar shape of the day now unfolding, the sheer contrariness of its promptings was what most surprised him, let alone his willingness to obey them. Biking into the country was something he'd never yearned to do, since even in its more indirect manifestations rurality held no allure for him. That was one of the reasons he stayed with Tom, because as yet his lover had evinced not the slightest desire to shuck off their shared carapace of urbanism in favour of horses and muddy walks. Finding himself pedalling onwards without a map through the sultriness of a late morning in northern Sussex, how was all of a sudden neither threatening nor particularly rebarbative. Ordinarily the least curious person in the world when it came to wanting to find out where roads led or what lay over the brow of the next hill, he was content nevertheless to let the yellow Muddy Fox carry him where it chose, trusting to some mystery of discretion among the glittering spokes and newly oiled cogs to decide when their mutual organism should achieve a suitable pause.

Clammy sweat on his thighs and shoulders and some dustiness in the mouth made him stop at last to swig water under a stand of trees at the top of a ridge. The number of passing cars seemed suddenly to increase, all of them, he noted, turning down the same side road a few yards on. Following in their wake, up another slope, past solemn-looking girls in peaked helmets on horseback, he came out above what looked like a fairground, with the sun glancing off ranked car bonnets behind a cluster of tents, the noise of an amplified voice barking over a tannoy and riders zigzagging up and down among jumps and poles, while over the bright orange bouncy castle in one corner of the swarming field children clambered shrieking. The bike, he reasoned with himself, would take him down there whether he wanted it or not, and soon enough he turned in through the opened gate alongside the trailing cars, to find himself checked almost at once by a red-faced woman in a voluminous pair of Union Jack bermudas, rattling a bucket.

'Yes, sorry,' she said, as if anticipating his protest, 'but it's a pound for cyclists. For the organ fund.'

Nonplussed, Cal asked: 'What, like kidney donors or something?'

She laughed gustily. 'No, love, the *church* organ. Needs a new blower.' She winked at him. 'If you know what that is!' and went off again into guffaws as he scrabbled, embarrassed, inside his rucksack for the money.

'You look as if you could do with a drink,' said the woman, all of a sudden solicitous. 'There's a beer tent over the other side, and Mrs Millichip and the others are doing salad lunches and ploughmen's by the gymkhana. Park your bike against that far fence, I should, it'll be quite safe there.'

On other occasions Cal might have found something intrusive and presumptuous in this desire to take care of him. Now it seemed entirely in order. Parking where he was told, he started to amble, pleasantly directionless, across the big field, among the trestle stalls full of pot plants and little cellophane-wrapped bags of home-made biscuits and sweets, the tombola with its rows of ticketed bottles graded according to their height, the opulent cake display under a striped awning, and the placard inviting him to guess the number of beans in a jar. He thought, by inevitable if bizarre association, of when he and Tom had been at Pride on Clapham Common last year, only this was somehow nicer because there as nobody here who knew him and he was quite alone amid the strangeness of it all, invisible apparently. No one seemed inclined to acknowledge his alien body, clad in its redundant signifiers of a thin grey vest and a tight sheating of Lycra, and he felt himself begin to absorb that quality of weightless disinvolvement with anything but the demands of an immediate present, a sensation he'd hitherto associated with being on holiday, always somewhere else than England.

Passing through the fair, he came at last to a small gate, pushed it open and walked on into a big, scrubby field strewn with tussocks of nettles and old grey cowpats, where one or two picnickers had spread rugs under the lee of the hedge. At the further end there rose up a long, bulky house of rust-coloured brick with a tall roof and yellow stone pillars gripping the space between long windows. In front of it a flagged terrace gave on to an expanse of lawn which seemed at length to become the very field in which Cal stood. As he drew nearer, the ground in front of him suddenly dropped away to a ditch with a walled embankment below the lawn, by which he was as appropriately surprised as ever its Georgian designer must have intended.

'And that's as far as you're coming, I'm afraid,' said a female voice somewhere beyond, to his left. 'Otherwise you'll have to go round and come all the way up through the park. And they'll ask you for money.'

Cal, taking off his shades to search with his eyes, found at length the figure of a girl in a blue dress sitting in a deckchair under the lime tree at the very edge of the lawn.

'They took a quid off me back there,' he laughed.

'Oh, I expect they'll have cleaned you out by the end of the afternoon, that's the general idea,' said the girl, leaning forward and staring hard at him.

She couldn't have been much more than fourteen or fifteen, yet there was a knowingness in her amused gaze Cal found slightly unsettling. He'd be better off down on the grass, he thought, and flopped into a safish patch between some thistles, taking care to cross his legs.

'I told them I'd help with the teas at four, but I don't really want to,' said the girl. 'We live here, you see, so one's sort of done it all before.'

'That must be nice,' ventured Cal politely.

'What?'

'Living in a home like this.'

She laughed softly, peering forward at him out of the shade across the ditch as though trying to find something in his face. 'You don't honestly mean that, do you?'

'No, I just said it for something to say.'

'Well, promise me you'll never say that sort of thing again. Because it's only half nice living here. Anyway, I don't when I can help it, I just came down for half-term to be with the parents so they wouldn't feel – you know – threatened.'

'Why should they? Feel threatened, I mean.'

The girl shifted a trifle uncomfortably. 'Oh, just because.'

'Go on, because what?' insisted Cal ruthlessly. 'It's funny talking to you like this from the other side of a ditch full of stinging nettles.'

'It's called a ha-ha,' said the girl with slight peevishness.

'So are lots of other things,' retorted Cal, aware now that he was beginning to wind her up and somewhat enjoying the process. He uncrossed his legs. 'Come on, tell me why your parents feel threatened.'

'Because of people like you,' she answered quietly, her eyes narrowing.

Cal laughed. 'You're joking! I'm about as threatening as a marshmallow.'

'I don't mean you personally, I mean . . .' She tossed back her hair in impatience. 'This is just pointless, I don't know why we started this conversation.'

'We didn't, you did. Over the ha-ha. "Actually it's called a ha-ha." '

'I didn't say "actually", and by the way, like most people you're useless at doing a posh accent.'

Instead of flouncing off as he half expected, she came and sat down on the edge of the wall, her white, freckled legs finding a foothold in the crooked brickwork. The awkwardness in her big-boned face and untidy fair hair put Cal at his ease. Had she been more conventionally attractive he'd almost certainly have got up and walked away. As it was, her nonchalant directness of engagement seemed entirely consistent with the day's mood.

'It's because you don't know what a ha-ha is,' she said, 'that's why they feel threatened.'

'You expect me to believe that?'

'Gosh, you're so literal, aren't you? Don't you know what I mean? People who talk about stinging nettles.'

'What should I have called them then?'

'Just nettles. And it's not a home, it's a house. A home is for old people to die in.'

'Okay, how old are your parents? No, don't tell me, I don't really want to know.' Momentarily enthralled, Cal sat upright out of the calculatedly indecent sprawl he'd adopted earlier. 'So what you're saying is – correct me if I'm wrong – that your mum and dad don't want anyone who's dead common, or even just common like me, hanging round the house. The home, sorry. Unless they pay two quid or whatever, for half an hour a week in the summer to see two rooms with red ropes all over them.'

She nodded approvingly.

'And that frightens them? So they're hiding under the chairs in the lounge until we've all buggered off home.'

'Something like that. Only my mother has to present the cups at the end of the gymkhana.'

'Assuming I know what that is, which I don't. So you're not going to invite me across the ha-ha and give me a glass of a sherry or a g. and t. Actually I could quite fancy a g. and t.'

'There, you said it that time.'

'What?'

'Actually. And no, I'm not going to ask you in.'

'I wasn't fishing for an invite, as it happens. Old houses don't interest me much.'

'But you said . . .'

'I was just being tactful, you knew that.' By now thoroughly relaxed, Cal smiled indulgently at her. 'I'd hate to live any-where like this, full of dust and junky furniture and windows which don't open properly.'

A little silence hung itself between them as the girl, seeming not to have heard his last remark and swinging her white-espadrilled feet against the brickwork, stared intently at him once more as if looking for something which should provide a needed clue. All of a sudden she had found it.

'You're gay, aren't you?' she announced with a sort of triumph in the discovery.

'Does it show?'

'Nobody in Sussex wears a vest like that, and those shorts are a dead giveaway. And that rucksack. And the way you sit, like somebody waiting to have their photo taken.'

Exhilarated by her aptness, Cal burst out laughing. 'You're just saying that because I trashed your house. I suppose now I've got to say "God, you're sophisticated" or something.'

'But it's true, isn't it?' she persisted. 'You are. Gay.'

Cal shrugged. 'If it's that important to you. It's not a thing I get asked very often.' Shaking his head, he watched her feet swaying to and fro along the moss-blotched wall. 'This is just so weird I can't believe,' he muttered, as the girl, in the same unpremeditated fashion as she had come and sat down opposite him, suddenly hoisted herself up again and returned to the deckchair. Reaching beneath it, she pulled out a book with a faded red cover, which she carried towards him with a faintly ceremonious air.

'Now,' she said, 'I'm going in to have some lunch. But before I do I've got to give you this. As a present.'

She might be seriously crazy, thought Cal. You read about people going bananas living in these old houses. Fancying it might be just as well to accept without demur, he moved forward to take the book from her, for all the world as if she were handing him a prize.

'It's *Cranford*,' she informed him, 'so funny. No, really, so sweet. And a bit sad.' Then, without another word, she ran off, flustered and ungainly, across the lawn, on to the terrace and through the open door into the house.

Briefly Cal wondered whether to clamber up, as he might so easily have done, over the edge of the wall and slip the book back under the chair. Instead, out of a vague respect, he tucked it inside his rucksack, that rucksack she'd been so alert in marking as a definer, and started meditatively to open his sandwiches, finding himself hoping she might return. He couldn't remember when anybody had ever spoken to him like that, without the least limiting frame of politeness, as if their immediate candour with each other were justified by some kind of ancient intimacy. She hadn't, for her own purposes, needed to know his name, what he did or where he came from, and having satisfied herself on the single point in him which appeared to arouse her curiosity, she had, spontaneously as it seemed, handed him a book, regardless of whether or not he was likely to be interested in it. 'Say funnee,' he mimicked her to himself under his breath, 'nay, rahllee. And say saird.'

What nagged at the edges of his enjoyment of the whole bizarre encounter was how on earth he should find a way of describing how it felt to Tom. If it came to that, the entire afternoon seemed to have in it less and less of anything at all likely to prove accountable when he got home. Surrender, Cal decided, was the best policy, as it had been beside the ha-ha, and while he moved from stall to stall, his waiter's anonymity still shielding him from too much attention being paid to his vest, as worn by nobody in Sussex, and the dead-giveaway shorts, he felt once again that sense of comfortable remoteness experienced earlier, a tourist's agreeably contained solitude mixed with his own insouciant reluctance to want anything offered here or desire those who presented it. Thus detached, he bought a ticket for the tombola, absent-mindedly sucked at an iced lolly till it dribbled off the stick, and fished incompetently for plastic ducks with a wire ring. At the Test-Your-Strength, encouraged by the same woman in the Union Jack bermudas who had waylaid him with the joke about the organ-blower and now cried 'Come on, Arnie, get those biceps working!' he swung the mallet with ease to knock the metal block to the top of the taut wire, and for gaining a careless triple won a jar of jam. Accepting it amid a little ripple of applause, Cal noticed the white gummed label on the side certifying that it was home-made, and realised that if he was to jettison so incongruous a trophy alongside the book, both must be deposited as far away from here as possible, preferably in one of the bins outside Clapham Junction station, where only the most malign of mischances would cause someone to recognise a dog-eared edition of *Cranford* or the legend 'Gooseberry. A. M. Hopkins, June, 1995'.

Beyond the beer tent, to which, for various reasons, he decided to give a wide berth, the riders were crowding into the far meadow as if in response to the inexorable voice, female and patrician, rapping out findings and exhortations to the scattered onlookers. A round-face child in a brown helmet, dismounting niftily from a grey pony, gave it him to hold before racing off among he straw bales to find the friend to whom she had lent a riding crop. 'He's perfectly all right with strangers,' she announced as Cal gingerly took the reins, 'only try not to let him eat anything, otherwise he'll be useless in the obstacle race.' So Cal stood there with the not unpleasing smells of Stockholm tar and equine sweat tickling his nostrils as the pony, swishing its tail and snorting occasionally, eyed him with the peculiar been-there-done-that expression by which horses make you appreciate the infinite courtesy their patience entails, and the imperious tannoy proclaimed: 'Caroline Molesworth on Dancing Queen, five faults . . . next is Sarah Pauling on Oscar . . . I've been asked to tell the owner of a green Renault Espace, registration number . . . Apparently the balloons from today's meet at Foxton are coming over in our direction, but I've been assured by Mrs Thursfield that they're all far too high up to frighten the horses.'

Only afterwards, when the moon-faced child, crop in hand, had sprung back into the saddle and taken off at a brisk trot towards the starting line and Cal was craning upwards towards the broadcast scatter of balloons across the afternoon's blatant sky, did he begin to wonder why she'd assumed he would do as she asked and hold the horse, without the slightest sense of a favour requested. Maybe, he reasoned, thinking of the older girl, the one in the blue dress dangling her freckled legs over the ha-ha wall, it was something people did round here. Instead of wearing Diesel vests they made assumptions. Feeling once again that altogether the wrong assumptions might be developed as a result of his presence in the beer tent, he settled instead for a cup of tea.

Its sides open to let the breeze stir the edges of the paper cloths covering the tables and of the little mock lace doilies under the plates of scones and rock cakes, the tea tent was loud with women suddenly falling upon Cal as if he had wandered in after years of unexplained absence. Two of them placed him in a corner, close to where the others were cutting sandwiches behind a screen, and one, small and sharp-eyed, taking his order, concluded by matter-of-factly saying: 'Better have your name in case I give it all to someone else, I'm getting dreadfully absent-minded this afternoon.'

Without a thought, Cal replied 'Christopher,' and there now, he had done it, uttered as if instinctively the name even Tom never dared to use, and she gave it him back, 'Christopher,' with a little nod, as if she thought that would do nicely. Behind the screen to one side of him he heard her chatting among the sandwich-cutters, perfectly unaware, as it seemed, that she must be audible to him.

'You've lost weight, Marion. Hasn't she? Hasn't Marion lost weight?'

'Twelve pounds. And I was telling Angela it's been only a few weeks since I started properly.'

'There's some more of that mayonnaise in that little tub there, he'll like that, I expect.'

'On his own, is he? Looked a nice lad when he came in.'

'Doesn't leave much to the imagination though, does he? Straight off of *Gladiators* in that outfit.'

'That's just what I thought. Or like that fireman who was on *Blind Date*, do you remember, and got off with that coloured girl and they went on a trip to Portugal together.'

'Except this one doesn't look the type that's going to be your toyboy, Janet.'

'Chance'd be a fine thing. He knows how to say please and thank you anyway. Better than Mrs Fairley's boy, that Barry, do you remember? Went to London for two weeks and came back a year later wearing a skirt. Claire saw him in Safeway at the less-than-ten-items and she said "Mum," she said, "I hardly knew where to look." But this one seems nice enough. There, give him the big piece, he'll eat it all. Do you know, when I asked him his name and he said "Christopher" he went all red, it was ever so sweet.'

'You want to take them home when they're like that, don't you?'

After this, of course, they all had to come round the screen and have another look at Cal, and he sat there, a complaisant cynosure, sipping his tea (from a real cup, he noted with approval) while they quizzed him about being a waiter in London and the famous people who came into the restaurant, and brought him a bit of Angela's special cake she was really keeping for when everyone had gone home, but Christopher could have some now, couldn't he, to put him on his way, because they honestly couldn't believe he was going to bike it on a hot afternoon like this, and wherever did he get his energy from, that's what Marion wanted to know, but he must come down and see them all again next year and maybe in the meantime, Janet suggested, they could all make a day of it in London, do some shopping, take in a show, *Miss Saigon* or something, and have a nice supper at the restaurant afterwards and he'd be there, wouldn't he, to point out who was who.

On his way back towards the station, feeling unbecomingly bloated by their relentless tending, he amused himself by imagining the scene as he sought to decode to them the mysteries of chowder, coulis and magret, while André the black dance student hovered with the Chardonnay and tight-arsed Dale the Australian with attitude tried not to notice when they asked for more of the olive bread. Already the scenario was perilous enough for him to imagine running on to the pavement as they materialised laughing and expectant outside the window, to warn them, with every reserve of his compassion, to go somewhere else where tapenade and pecorino shavings had never been heard of.

There was a good twenty minutes before the train arrived, and Cal had started to resign himself to sitting alone amid the platform's five o'clock sultriness when he remembered the book. Pulling it from the rucksack, he turned the opening leaves more for the sake of occupation than out of any specific curiosity. An odd damp smell rose from the pages as he riffled them over, almost a green scent like something off a tree. Idly he began reading: 'Cranford. Chapter I. Our Society. In the first place, Cranford is in possession of the Amazons'. He had not closed the book when the train at length hove into view.

He had still not closed it by the time they reached Gatwick, and was farther than ever from doing so at East Croydon. As always, his Walkman was indispensable, and Miss Betsy Barker's Alderney cow in dark grey flannel and Miss Deborah Jenkyns in her little bonnet like a jockey-cap partied with hedonistic abandon to 'Keep On Climbin' ' (Fade 2 End Mix) while Cal, though less and less certain of why exactly he needed to prick on through successive chapters of a story which seemed largely concerned with elderly spinsters in a small town trying not to call a spade a spade and making themselves ridiculous in the process, grew increasingly determined to persevere. He'd always been a slow, unwilling reader, yet perhaps for that very reason the novel's insidious authority of detail worked more easily upon him. He couldn't help laughing at the cow and at Martha saying to Miss Matty: 'Well, ma'am, I should say you were not far short of sixty: but folks' looks is often against them,' at poor Peter dragging up in Deborah's bonnet and shawl and cuddling the pillow like a baby and at Mr Mulliner who looked 'like a sulky cockatoo'. He thought he could have fancied Jem Hearn the joiner 'making three-and-sixpence a day, and six foot one in his stocking-feet' and smiled approvingly at Martha resolutely declaring: 'I like lads best.' Not necessarily given to sentiment, he felt something like a pang when Mr Holbook died and Miss Matty, having ordered her widow's caps, exclaimed: 'God forbid! that I should grieve any young hearts.'

Only when Cal stepped from the train at Clapham Junction did he acknowledge how effectively such absorption had prevented him from confronting the problem of what was to be said to Tom. It was around half past six, and he might simply

have sidled into the flat in an atmosphere of no-questions-
asked and started up a 'how was your day, darling' interrog-
ation which would almost certainly result in Tom announcing
that there'd been time, after all, to get the new blades and
how he'd got this *wicked* pair which he'd just *had* to go
straight to Kensington Gardens to try out and how there
were these three drop dead gorgeous Spanish guys there in
psychedelic all-in-ones like they were a team or something,
who etc., etc. As it was, Cal, pulling up the hill towards the
common, sensed the beginnings of an odd, brooding appre-
hensiveness, rooted in something that felt like guilt only
wasn't exactly.

At the crossing by the Avenue he turned and started heed-
lessly down the path along the edge of the little wood.
Shadows were lengthening among the trees, but the grass was
still dotted with a few late sunbathers, some of whom he
thought at a glance to recognise. From the bushes came an
unmistakable laugh he knew for Matt's, the last person at
this moment he could have wished to meet, so he quickened
his speed, veering away on to the open sward beyond, with
its tremendous northward sweep closed by clustered plane
trees around the roofs of Old Town and the slate-grey church
spire. Halfway across, avoiding the cricketers and bouncing
dogs, he stopped and flung himself on to the dry, scratchy
turf, suddenly overmastered with tiredness and the fear of
going home.

Solitary, hugging his knees, his gaze fixed gloomily on
nothing in particular, he wondered what language he would
use for telling Tom about Angela's special cake, the jar of
gooseberry jam, Mrs Fairley's Barry, the balloons which Mrs
Thursfield assured them wouldn't frighten the horses, the
nettles in the ha-ha and his giveaway shorts. How was he
going to finish *Cranford* in any case? Books for them both
were merely tiresome space-hoggers, and apart from a small
stack of style bibles used as a strategic marker to complete
the visual impact they had laboured so hard to achieve in the

living area and a clutch of recipe collections in the kitchen, the flat was mercifully free of such swarming impertinences.

Now Cal felt like a smuggler, spiriting into a domain of hitherto inviolate modernity inhabited by a brace of young males the work of an old, dead woman, her discourse half incomprehensible to him, the remoteness of her preoccupations from his own almost planetary in its extent. How could he tell Tom that having spent the day at a church fe–te somewhere in Sussex, in the company, almost exclusively, of wives and daughters, he had enjoyed himself without experiencing any special wish to repeat the occasion, but that some half-veiled ordinance given to him by the day's events meant that he had absolutely to establish what happened at the end of *Cranford*?

At first it seemed as if he need scarcely have bothered. Tom, as foretold, had found his new blades, got to the sloping walk in Kensington Gardens to show them off, and instead of three Spaniards had met two seriously cute Sicilian boys called Tony and Ludovico who worked at Hackett's in Sloane Square and had this incredible technique they were going to show him next week, and Cal must come along too because they really wanted to meet him, and Tony had a friend in Paul Smith Accessories who'd got these brilliant socks at a discount which had been in that fashion spread in last month's *Attitude*, and . . . Listening, Cal perceived how impossible it must be to say anything about today that would make sense, even to himself, and decided regretfully that he might as well paper everything over with a few cosmetic lies. Accordingly, when Tom, pausing to draw breath, asked how was Brighton, he merely supplied the vaguest trifle of a few hours with nothing arresting enough in them to justify detailed recollection, and this appeared to answer the purpose, doubtful to Cal as that was.

After supper he unpacked his rucksack, taking care to put his unused beach towel in the laundry basket and feeling thankful that a recent heavy reinforcement of his tan on a sunbed at the gym meant that Tom was unlikely to ask inconvenient questions about parts of him which might otherwise have stayed obstinately pale under the notional marine glare. Thinking, then, that he might slip the gooseberry jam into the back of a cupboard without attracting notice, he was a shade too late in getting to the kitchen, for here, at his shoulder, was Tom asking: 'What the hell's that stuff?'

Cal didn't turn. 'Oh, just something this woman was selling off a stall outside a church. I bought it so as not to upset her.'

'You're too bloody soft-hearted, you are. Let's have a look.'

'No, I'm putting it in the cupboard.'

'Hang about, let's . . .'

But there, as Tom reached over to grab the jar, it fell from Cal's hands and smashed on the baked terracotta of the kitchen floor. Sinking to his knees like a mourner, as if desperate to salvage anything of what remained, Cal glared up at the sheepish Tom.

'Just a heap of green goo,' said the culprit defensively.

'It was my gooseberry jam. Home-made.' Cal's voice had softened to a furious whisper. 'You broke my fucking pot of gooseberry jam.'

'I'm going to shower,' was all Tom could find to say. 'Maybe we can do the Two Brewers before we go over to Brixton.'

Cal, staring at the glistening debris on the floor, silently shook his head and started reaching about for a dustpan.

Afterwards, knowing Tom would take ages in the shower, he got out *Cranford* from under the sofa where it lay hidden, and carried it into the bedroom to read for a furtive half-hour against the noise of Tom's desultory singing and clattering. Cal's anger had subsided almost at once. Tom would never apologise directly, and only offered token amends for anything. He, on the other hand, always forgave, knowing himself to be the stronger, and tonight in any case magnanimity was more opportune than having to explain any further the totemic import of 'Gooseberry. A. M. Hopkins'. He was careful, however, when the bathroom door clicked open, not just to slide *Cranford* under his side of the mattress where the fall of the duvet neatly masked it, but to sit with his back to the door, shoulders hunched with a suitable moroseness. Thus Tom could flop across the bed behind him, kiss him penitently on the neck and squeeze his hand.

Without turning round, Cal murmured: 'Say funnee. Nay, rahlee. And a bit sad. Tell me what I'm going to wear tonight.'

Naked except for his socks, Tom went to the wardrobe and browsed exuberantly among the hangers. For an instant or two Cal watched the play of muscle up and down his back and flanks, almost envying the determination in the movement of his hands along the rail and the whole taut confidence of the body thus viewed.

"Jem Hearn, he said at least, 'six foot one in his stocking-feet.'

'What's that?'

'Nothing.'

'You're weird tonight, my baby, seriously.'

'I said tell me what I'm wearing.'

Tom was right, he was completely out of it, and made no very strenuous effort for the rest of the evening to climb back in. At the Brewers they met Garry and Mark just home from Sydney and got introduced to Jamie's boyfriend who had made this fantastic promo video for a new band who were going to kick Ant & Dec into next week. At the Fridge everyone was there, Damian whom Tom knew from the studio, the rangy New Zealander who'd been so on to them both at Venom the other week, and the DJ from Iron Bar with the teeth. Yet all the time, up and down the grooves of Cal's fretful, unslaked imagination, ran the train which killed poor Captain Brown, pussy eating Mrs Forrester's collar and sicking it up again and Miss Matty rolling her ball under the bed because she was afraid somebody would catch her 'by the last leg'. It was only two o'clock when he told Tom he wanted to go home, and was embarrassed by his lover immediately volunteering to leave with him.

On the air hitting them smartly as they tumbled out on to the pavement he thought to catch again something of that green scent which had assailed him this morning as he sat at the window with his coffee. For some time they walked in silence, while Cal felt Tom, troubled, look at him askance. For Christ's sake, thought Cal, don't ask me to tell you what it is I know. Putting his hands up to his lover's face once they were inside the car, he whispered: 'I like lads best.' Tom's eyes in the darkness were brilliant with incomprehension, but at this moment he knew better than to speak. When they got home and had bundled monosyllabically into bed, he went off to sleep with an emphatic heaviness derived as much from natural discretion as from the fatigue induced that afternoon's blading with the cute Sicilians.

Cal, of course, did not sleep. Waiting until he caught the steady rhythm of Tom's breathing beside him, he twitched the book from its hiding place, eased himself out of bed and tiptoed along the corridor to make himself comfortable on the sofa. Silence within the house was absolute. Nothing stirred in the windless night beyond. For a time he read intently, almost with desperation, then, suddenly frightened at the noise the pages made when he turned them, he allowed the stillness momentarily to possess him before he picked up the book again with a sort of shame at having permitted himself even momentarily to abandon it.

'Babe, are you okay?'

Tom stood there now in the open doorway, the clean, unquestionable line of his body looking as if formed out of the very light it obstructed.

'What are you doing?'

'Just reading.'

'Reading?'

'Yeah.'

Tom came and put an arm round him. The only thing he

could have done, Cal realised, and kissed him softly before he could say: 'I'm sorry. About the jam.'

'It's all right, just go back to bed, I'll come in a bit.'

But a faint paleness of morning was already in the room when Cal himself slipped back beside the sleeping Tom. An extraordinary wave of compassion went over him as he settled down beside the other man's warm nakedness and ran a hand in consolation gingerly over his outstretched arm, fearful of waking him. *Cranford* was still unfinished. Before shutting it for the night he'd taken a pen from beside the telephone and written his full name in it, Christopher Adam Lamb. He must protect Tom, he realised, from wanting to know why. God forgive that he should grieve any young hearts. In the grey half-light the starkness of things, a sock, a pair of boots, a towel over a chair, began to declare itself. 'Perhaps tomorrow,' he said gently to his sleeping lover, 'I'll buy myself some pyjamas.'

What Avi Told Me

Every night the Bernsteins, who lived at the end of our road, wept over their son. Surely not every night, I objected in the literal fashion of adolescence, but yes, Mum said, it was every night, Sandra Dobin told her, who lived next door to them, you could hear the Bernsteins in the kitchen weeping. It's a thing Jews do (you're not Jewish so you wouldn't understand), they weep a lot when their children don't turn out quite as expected. It wasn't made clear to me what Tony Bernstein had done wrong or how he'd failed to shoulder the accumulated baggage of hopes with which his parents loaded him. The fact was that on summer evenings in Ashbourne Avenue, Sandra Dobin, sitting in the conservatory, could hear the Bernsteins quietly but persistently sobbing together as they sat at the kitchen table.

Now and then during those June weeks when I was doing my GCSEs I'd see Mr Bernstein coming out of the Underground station, hunched and lugubrious-looking, a distinctly old-fashioned figure in his Prince of Wales check three-piece which seemed quite eccentrically inappropriate to the weather. 'Don't worry, Mr Bernstein,' I wanted to say, 'it's not the end of the world, even if your pallid, hollow-eyed son, with his white jeans and that manky-looking baseball cap which has BEAR CUBS picked out on the front (only it's lost the Band weirdly says EAR CUBS), has done something you daren't even apply a name to. There are lots of other

Jewish boys who'll give you back your faith in human nature. Me, for instance.'

I was massively into Me at that time, partly because nobody seemed disposed to say 'Don't' and partly by virtue of having found a way of being so which wouldn't desperately annoy other people. In our youth group, which met each week at someone else's house, we'd discussed Abraham's bargain with God over the wrongdoers. You didn't know Avi was short for Avraham? Well, it is, and I felt that was who I had to be. 'Live up to your name, boychik,' Dad had said at my barmitzabah, so it was easy enough for me to imagine being Abraham compassionately haggling with God for a few right-eous among the sinners. That was me, standing there in a bathtowel on some stony plain in the Negev, waving my arms at the sky. Okay, god, if you can't give me fifty, we'll say twenty. Fair enough, I'll settle for ten. You know, God, for someone in your position you drive one hell of a bargain.

Except that of course I wouldn't call Him God to His face. New teachers at school used routinely to ask why it was that some Jewish boys wrote the word as 'G-d' when everybody else in the class gave Him the regulation triple letters. I just smiled politely, the way my parents taught me. 'There's no point in explaining, Avi,' said Mum, 'they don't understand. Just make sure you always do it, that's all.' She didn't even need to say 'promise', that was the kind of boy she had convinced herself I was turning out to be.

The school I attended had been specially chosen by my parents because of its celebrity throughout north London as the first ever to admit Jews with no questions asked. I'd got two cousins there. Cousins, you gather, are what all Jews have, and your parents, from them moment you're born, run you against them like professional greyhounds. It wasn't exactly difficult to compete with either of mine. Ashley got slung out halfway through the Third Form for pulling a knife on some mouthy kid in the playground, while Howard was a bespectacled grotesque who surfed the Internet like the

Flying Dutchman and became Hon. Sec. of the Star Trek Appreciation Society.

Ominously meanwhile I grew in grace, learned how to carry an umbrella and asked awkward questions of visiting MPs about secret British defence links with Syria and Iran and the Foreign Secretary's support for the PLO. 'I suppose they'll make you head boy next,' said Howard drily on one of the few occasions when I felt I could risk being seen with him, but they'd had Jews the two previous years so, as a kind of ethnic Buggins's turn, it went instead to a hairy, good-humoured Asian named Sandeep with a gold watch and teeth like piano keys. On Prize Day, however, a total dude in my new Hugo Boss, I shook the Lord Mayor's hand and looked him straight in the eye with that particular kind of sincerity my American uncle on his last visit had striven to teach me. Coming away with Dr Conquest's Gold Medal, the Livery-men's Distinguished Service Award and the Mortimer English Prize, I had a general sense that now if I went to the Negev and waved my arms about, God, all three letters of him, simply couldn't refuse.

Mum and Dad had never been altogether happy with me choosing English for A level. They didn't say anything, of course – ours was, officially at least, a happy home – but for reasons I couldn't then fathom they were continuously uneasy. After parents' evenings, which should have been a breeze, they came back to garland me with the plaudits of my history teachers or with the French department's recommendation that I be allowed to go to Montpellier for a summer school (Mum, waiting politely for Mr Ferguson to finish, implied that this was out of the question simply for dietary reasons) and then Dad would say, pausing to clear his throat as if having to negotiate a major unpleasantness: 'Oh, and Mr Brownynge says you're getting on nicely in your English.'

I sort of guessed what the trouble was. We had plenty of books in the house, Primo Levi, George Steiner, Elie Wiesel, you name it, my parents were no slouches when it came to serious reading, but the notion that I should choose to spend two years engaged with a subject which had no perceptible relationship to any career other than teaching was always one that unsettled them. You're the sort of cultivated Gentile who thinks Jews spend their leisurehours studying Walter Benjamin and playing the violin. It's not like that in NW11 and still less like it in Stanmore and Hendon, supposing it ever was. We may *listen* to the Amadeus String Quartet or a lecture by Isaiah Berlin but we're not meant to want to *be* like them. Seeing me writing essays on *Middlemarch* was something my parents learned to put up with, yet just because they never said anything to me about it, I knew that it was a stone in the shoe for them both.

Maybe I'd only chosen English because of Adam Bassano, glamorously Levantine, captain of the second XI for cricket, with a sister everyone said looked like Julia Roberts and agreeably drawling accents which were emphatically not those of Temple fortune. Adam was what's called a diamond geezer, one hundred per cent what-you-see-is-what-you-get, and by the end of the Fifth Year I was starting to prefer his company to that of the peasants with whom I ran the Junior Jewish Society and the lunchtime minyan. There was something protective in his urbanity, an amiable pseudo-indolence of the kind which allowed him constantly to astound his teachers with essays whose precision and fluency justified them being handed in a fortnight after the deadline. So I'd sit at the back of the room with Adam and wait for him to blink heavy eyelids and mutter something about verification, with sundry 'likes' and 'you knows' giving the illusion of spontaneity, before the mildly irritated Mr Brownynge, in his raspberry socks and tortoiseshell frames, turned to me and said caustically: 'As so often, Avi, we rely on you to supply us with something approaching a *coherent* answer.'

Adam showed no resentment at my enquire-within facility, and in that sense I suppose we formed a double act, his deliberate torpor agreeably enhancing my glibness. Once or twice, however, the intensity of his perceptions left me stranded, offering nothing in the way of friendly advantage on which I could seize to impress the enduringly sardonic Brownynge, a man whom another of our contemporaries described as 'drowning his porridge in sulphuric acid'. We were talking in class, I remember, about the ending of an American short story in which the heroine and her best friend are lunching at the fish restaurant under Grand Central Station, and while they're both ordering she understands that her fiancé and the best friend have been seeing each other, simply by virtue of the fact that the other woman orders a beer.

The nature of this particular *paerçu* puzzled me to the extent that I dismissed it as downright pretentiousness. Okay, if they'd said what kind of beer it was and she knew that was the boyfriend's favourite, fair enough, but it was just the ordering which, so we were required to believe, made her guess that he was cheating on her. Some of the others, to my slightly irked surprise, didn't agree. Animated all of a sudden – and now Brownynge's face crinkled into the nearest version he could manage of indulgent amusement – Adam sat up, opened his eyes and turned towards me a glance full of patient reproof.

'Listen, you don't have to spell these things out, for Christ's sake. They happen all the time, like somebody having an extra pair of eyes or something, sort of programmed to see what isn't there.'

'But it *is* there,' I insisted obtusely, 'only that's not the way to make us understand.'

'So how are you going to get it across?' said Adam. 'Have the pair of them talking about it over the smoked haddock? Oh yeah, so convincing, I don't think!'

'No, but . . .'

Brownynge watched the pair of us like some Gibbonian emperor preparing to raise or lower a deciding thumb before a crowd in the arena.

'Look, it's a question of body language maybe,' Adam said, as if spelling out the issue to a child, 'or just because the way people see things isn't always like, you know, what's in front of them. Jesus, you're so literal, I hadn't realised.' The rest of the class cracked up with laughter, less at me than at his exasperation. 'Like everything's got to have a label on it. Get real, Avi.'

He meant it kindly, as always. The irony of all this was that I came from a family where nothing was ever discussed, because, it was believed, there was never any need. My parents, Dad in particular, cherished a curious but persistent notion of the Jewish household s one in which, since so much of life was preordained according to religious observance, the existence of doubts or even of the merest nuance on the gloss of an unquestionable righteousness could never be acknowledged. 'We're getting there,' he used to say – it was a preferred cliché – when we walked home together from shul or cleared the table after seder, and I felt somehow bidden to understand that part of the process of getting there was not talking about the sort of things the hapless Mr and Mrs Bernstein at number 47 must have felt compelled to discuss in the wake of pale-faced, earringed Tony's innominable wickedness.

I had cause to ponder some of this afresh when, halfway through my first year in the Sixth, Adam Bassano asked me to dinner. 'Come to dinner next Wednesday,' he said, meeting me in the corridor before morning assembly and patting my shoulder with that air of patrician encouragement which in anyone else would have been wholly insufferable. I was tongue-tied because nobody in my entire life had issued me with a dinner invitation. Seventeen-year-old boys don't, as a general rule, sit down to dine, even when their mothers put out a mat, a napkin and a knife and fork on the kitchen table, and add to this domestic *mise-en-scène* a plate of something hot. Instead of telling Adam not to be a toffee-nosed git and asking him to come up north and go with me to Carmeli's or Milk & Honey or one of the places down

Hampstead High Street where we could locate some well fit birds to go with the meal, I managed to stammer a 'yes', if only because he made it sound so grown up, as though we had suddenly leapt a decade and were out in the world with the trappings of adulthood scattered gratifyingly around us both.

Of course, I had to tell Mum. Dad was away on business in Tel Aviv (in north London, by the way, we pronounce it so that the last syllable rhymes with 'give'), which happened several times a year, so she was especially conscious of having at all costs to maintain the hallowed routines as if his absence somehow menaced their consistency. Once or twice I even heard her say 'We're getting there,' so that the formula might give the occasion a greater authenticity.

'Can I go to dinner at Adam's on Sunday?' I asked.

She smiled, indestructibly serene as she sorted out the wools for her tapestry cushion. 'Adam who? Oh yes, I remember Adam, he's that nice boy I met at the Summer Fair last year. Where do they live, darling?'

'Phillimore Gardens.'

Still smiling, yet preoccupied behind the smile, she asked: 'That's not round here, is it?'

'Erm, no, Kensington actually.'

Her features suddenly relaxed into seriousness. 'You're going to dinner in Kensington?'

'Well, yes, if that's all right.'

She paused for a moment, as if, unexpectedly, she'd found something which needed explaining, to me rather than to her.

'This Adam,' she said at length, 'his family are Jewish, aren't they?'

It amused me that from being 'that nice boy' he'd degenerated into 'this Adam' solely for living in Kensington.

'Oh yes, of course. And they keep kosher and everything.'

It was one of the earliest occasions on which I'd ever properly lied to my mother. Adam was indeed a Jew, but I was far from being assured that the Bassanos were specially strict in observing the dietary laws. The fib was a trifling one, perpetrated for the sake of an event I think I'd have crawled to in terminal decline, yet it trailed a slow fuse of far greater significance.

We arranged then that I should go to Kensington by the Underground, but that I was to come home in a taxi, for which Mum provided me with a twenty-pound note. I was to ring her as soon as I reached my destination and I must get back before midnight. All of this was determined without the least hint of harshness or menace, by the way. Uncertainties my mother might now and then experience: insecurity she never publicly acknowledged.

What's more, in some intuitive sense she'd been right about Kensington. The big white mansion in Phillimore Gardens was different from our house not just because it was older, with more floors and immeasurably grander rooms, but because the Bassanos contrived to inhabit it in a way I'd never come across before. Home in NW11 had, I now realise – and Phillimore Gardens first made me see this – a strangely unlived-in quality, as if all the furniture had arrived from somewhere else only the previous day and would shortly be carried out to a waiting van while we tottered to the station with our suitcases. You could say this had something to do with a race memory of pogroms and emigration and always having to be in readiness for a quick flit to some other town where, for the time being, Jews would be safe, but I don't think the explanation is so anthropologically simple.

The Bassanos, Adam and his sister Dinah (who really was a dead ringer for Julia Roberts) and their parents, lived in that house as if it had always been theirs from the moment when somebody in the 1860s, I don't know who, Thomas Cubitt perhaps, laid out the building plots at the back of Holland Park. Clean, well kept and handsome, the rooms possessed, as I gradually came to realise, an extraordinary feeling of occupation, intimated in even them most negligible detail, chair cushions intensely sat upon, a scatter of petals fallen from the big vase of roses on top of the piano, a pair of shoes under the hall table or an envelope which someone had torn open and then flung on to the sideboard in the dining room.

What such features created was the impression of an unfathomable ease and expansiveness from which the family, as it were, rose to greet me. Visually the four of them, taken as an ensemble and catching lustre from one another, appeared absolutely stunning, as if, I now like to think, they'd been waiting for Sargent to come and paint them. Under the drawing room's pools of mellowed light and shadow they had a kind of Mediterranean sheen and substance to them, florid and appetising, which both cowed and excited me. In the sound of their voices I caught a different confidence from my mother's, and some faintest of initial impulses made me want to know exactly what its source was. Of course, Adam had partly familiarised me with this already, but to hear it as a distinctive music, charging the air with new modulations and suspensions, devastated what little composure I had left.

The guests arrived and at length we went in to dinner. There were nine of us at table, including a thumping blonde schoolfriend of Dinah's who was half French and called Marie-Laure, an art historian from the Courtauld with a wife who wrote features for the *Daily Telegraph*, and an actor named Charles, a star in a recent TV adaptation of *Our Mutual Friend*. Care had evidently been taken to ensure that I should not be beguiled into eating whatsoever cleaveth the hoof but cheweth not the cud, but it was only after about half an hour, during which some utterly banal remark of mine about Channel Four had been gratifyingly hailed as if ripe for anthologising and I'd started to develop pressing sensations of now-happy-could-I-be-with-either-were-tother-dear-charmer-away for Dinah and Marie-Laure on each side of me, that I suddenly awoke to the astounding fact that apart from me and the Bassanos, everybody at the table was a Gentile.

I can't expect you to understand what this perception did

to me, and I shan't try to explain. For now, anyway. Perhaps not ever, except to somebody Jewish. Enough surely to say that in that moment I felt an oddly thrilling stab of guilt towards my mother and wondered almost wearily whether I should need to lie to her again. The only other thing you really need to know in order to appreciate this story properly is something that arose out of what Charles the actor and the *Daily Telegraph* woman opposite me were discussing as the pudding came on. Someone they knew, a fairly distinguished political journalist whose articles I'd occasionally read, had just left his wife for the female editor of a smart lifestyle magazine who gave her well-heeled friends a recommendation or two as to what to do with their rugs and their wallpaper.

'And did she know about Miranda?' I heard Charles ask.

'Oh, of course she knew,' said the *Telegraph*, 'or at any rate she soon found out.'

'Well, how exactly? They were pretty discreet about it to start off with.'

'I'll tell you how. Caroline was at breakfast and Bobby came down and sat there a bit and munched his toast. Then apparently he looked over towards the window and said: "We really ought to get these curtains changed." And in a split second Caroline thought: "My God, he's been seeing Miranda Phelps." '

'Just from Bobby noticing the curtains? That's brilliant!'

Staring at Adam, I wondered if he remembered the argument in Brownynge's lesson, but obviously he hadn't been listening. For whatever reason the idea of a wife realising that her husband was cheating on her simply by him suggesting that they needed new curtains scarcely seemed quite as implausible as it might have done last term. Or maybe this reaction was just primed by the atmosphere of the evening as a whole, with the hints it kept giving me of some hitherto untapped reserve of sophistication, novel and vast, like something the Bassanos could have drawn up by pulling a ring in one of the stones of their cellar floor or kept in bottles in the pantry.

A day or two afterwards Dad came home from Tel Aviv. As always on these occasions he quizzed me painstakingly on my reading, my prayers, my homework, whether I got back from school in time for the sabbath and on the I was doing for A/S-level Jewish History. Mum sat listening with her tapestry on her knee, now and then enhancing, with the aid of little approving clucks and nods, the picture of me he seemed so anxious to establish, that of a well-brought-up, modest, pious and diligent Jewish boy whose behaviour and achievements would always somehow vindicate a careful practice of the faith. Returning like this he invariably seemed, for a day or two, a trifle distant from us, as though the absence had lasted a year rather than a mere ten days. Mum told him some gossip she'd heard at shul about Shirley Rappaport's sister Jackie, who'd moved down to Chalk Farm and become a Christian after getting divorced. Listening, Dad gave a little shake of the head. 'Here's a statistic for you, Avi,' he said, 'though I know you don't like maths. Jewish families – real Jewish families – have the lowest divorce rate in Britain. Now did you know that?' I said I didn't know. Mum looked at him over her spectacles and smiled.

If only they could have guessed at the serpent they cherished as a son. For indeed that dinner in Phillimore Gardens had ruined me eternally. By slow degrees, becoming absorbed into Adam's family, getting a little hot for Dinah and even snogging her briefly at a crazy New Year's Eve party in Hammersmith with some boys they knew at St Paul's, listening to their mother describing the villa they'd rented in the Marche so that they could, as she put it, 'pop across to Pesaro for the Rossini' (I hadn't the least idea what she was talking about but it sounded magnificent), and watching entranced as Mr Bassano turned over his collection of Baroque drawings, I began to be another kind of Jew altogether from the one my parents thought walked up the hill from the Underground station, opened the gate and slipped the key into the lock of their front door. I started to understand how Jewishness might be a fact even amid the indefinite ethnicities of Kensington High Street, in a household which, though it drew the line at shellfish, scarcely jibbed at spaghetti alla carbonara, and jocularly portrayed itself as a 'country member' of the congregation at the Rutland Gate synagogue.

The secret prayer of every Gentile – even one as evolved as you – is that one day we'll all stop being Jewish. A friend of my uncle's, a war correspondent in Saigon at the end of the Vietnam War, once described to me the scene as he entered the city atop the first Vietcong tank. Wandering through the side streets he watched in amazement as all the South Vietnamese soldiers simply shucked off their uniforms on the pavement and in seconds became innocent know-nothing civilians. That's what you goyim hope we'll do, dump our Jewishness in a little crumpled heap and run away for ever, unmade by assimilation.

That this doesn't happen was what I learned in Phillimore Gardens. My parents had to grasp it as well, only the process would take far longer, perhaps never achieving the fulfilment I so idealistically projected. I made excuses for missing the youth group, I stopped wearing my kuppel and once at Cambridge I gave up attending shul. You'd think any of these might have been a signal for family despair, for the harps of Temple Fortune to be hung on willow trees, and for continuous weeping, of the sort which bedewed the wretched Bernstein boy, to break out by whatever waters flow amid the uplands beyond the North Circular, but with Mum and Dad it wasn't like that. They could have frosted me off or remonstrated openly or just pretended I didn't exist. Instead they seemed quietly to be waiting, as they've done ever since, for me to come back. I open the gate, I put the key in the lock of the front door, but they don't greet me as the Bassanos did that evening. I'm not Sargent coming to paint them. In fact it's not at all clear to them who I am.

Does that sound pathetic? Listen, I'll tell you something, something that happened last year, when I started on my postgraduate work and had to go to Israel to look at an archive in a house on the edge of Tel Aviv. It belongs to the widow of a scholar from Corfu named Samuel Nahmias, who collected Ladino romances from all over the Balkans and got away on a boat to Egypt just before the Italians invaded Greece. So I telephoned Mum from Cambridge to ask if she thought Dad would mind if I used the apartment.

'No, darling,' she answered a shade flatly, 'he won't mind.'

'I expect nothing's changed since we were there five years ago,' I said.

'Well, I wouldn't know, would I? I never did care for Tel Aviv.'

It was true: she hated travelling anyway and went to Jerusalem largely from duty, but seemed wholly without curiosity as to what the rest of Israel might look like. While I was still a decent Jewish boy I used to find this rather embarrassing.

'I'll pick up the keys when I'm home next week.'

'Yes, darling, you do that.'

Her lack of enthusiasm was in marked contrast to my father's surprisingly fervent admission that he wished he was coming with me. As it happened, I was delighted at the prospect of being on my own, and knew before I got there precisely how I intended to fill my hours. Dad's presence would only have cramped my style. Yet I felt him near me as soon as I unlocked the door, on the fifth floor of a building overlooking a stretch of waste ground like something used for army training, with a distant prospect, through the heat haze, of low dunes and an iron-grey blur of sea beyond. Someone, I didn't yet know who, plainly came in from time to time to dust, and there was a sense of hands making everything just so, as if in readiness for an imminent arrival – his, not mine. I'd been here before, of course, but I'd forgotten how cosy a space it was, how sat in, sprawled over, trodden upon, eaten off, if indeed I'd ever taken note of that earlier.

So every day I breakfasted on the little terrace overlooking the scrubland and the dusty carob trees by the roadside, and went off in a taxi to listen to Mrs Nahmias cackling over the scandals of wartime Alexandria before she unlocked the library, where I had to work in semi-darkness in order to allay her morbid horror of the precious archive decomposing in the sunlight. During the afternoon I'd go and find a girl on the beach, check out she wasn't Israeli, and get started with the same kind of single-mindedness I'd brought to the transliteration of Sephardi ballads only hours before.

The incident I wanted to tell you about – though honestly I don't think you'll understand what I mean – took place one morning when I was on my way to the archive. There was this Danish girl named Ebba with whom I'd fancied spending some time. She was working on some archaeological project up in the Galilee, but seemed to want to turn her researches down here into an extended pretext for being with me, and had more or less moved into the flat. Leggy and loose-boned, with a comically gloomy look in her massive green eyes, she was the laziest girl I'd ever met. We used to have a joke, because her family back in Denmark was grand and lived in a castle, which the Danes call *slot*, about Ebba being a slut from a slot. That was how I liked her, flopped down beside the overfilled ashtrays and coffee-cup rings on the bedside table, among the sheets we ought to have washed a week ago, with a half-finished book propped face down next to a snatch of yesterday's newspaper and a bottle of Lord gin horizontal on the carpet. Ebba helped me to make the flat even more inhabited than I found it at first, but the odd impression of *Gemütlichkeit* still haunted me, and I kept wondering when the unknown polisher and arranger would knock on the door.

That morning we slept late, and when I bundled out of bed it was already half past ten. Mrs Nahmias didn't like me staying beyond midday, when she had an early lunch and afterwards took an extended nap, so I quickly called a taxi, then began gathering up the notes I thought I'd need from under the piles of clothes and books where they lay buried. Leaving Ebba asleep (as, almost certainly, I should find her when I got back) and hurrying down to the waiting car, I realised that the papers had to be in a particular order if the best use was to be made of the hour at my disposal, part of which would no doubt have to be given over to the memory of her childhood in the Kerkyra ghetto on which Mrs Nahmias had embarked yesterday with the apparent idea that I'd be interested in writing it up.

The taxi bowled onwards as I rifled fretfully over my notes, having acknowledged too late that one essential transcription, a Bosnian variant of *El Conde Arnaldos*, had been left behind. Only after a while did it dawn on me that we were travelling by a completely different route from the one I usually took. The suburb in question seemed less frequented, its pavements wider, rather American-looking, with open plots of garden stretching down from the low-pitched houses, each with its carport and crazy-paved path.

Suddenly the cab started to slow and at length it came to a halt in front of a rambling bungalow with a hibiscus trained over a pergola covering the little terrace in front. I don't know exactly what I thought – probably that the driver needed to pick something up from here – but I was much too preoccupied with my papers at that moment to ask what the matter was. Then, hearing the door open, I watched a woman come out under the open and take a few steps down the path. I can remember, you see, precisely what she looked like, thin, reddish hair, dark earrings, a slightly gaunt but not unattractive face, and a green skirt with a kind of sash arrangement round the waist. Her pace quickened as she neared the car. She was smiling, I'd almost have said laughing as if in disbelief at something. Then she caught sight of me through the taxi's open window, raised shocked hands to her face and rushed back towards the safety of the house. That was the instant when the taximan chose to turn round. He wasn't my usual driver, I'd noted earlier, and now he laughed. 'But I made a mistake! I thought you were your father. It's where I usually bring him.' Peering at me over the back of the seat, he added: 'You look just like your father sitting there.' Then we drove on in silence to Mrs Nahmias's.

This is where you'd like me to say something along the lines of 'And then I realised everything Dad told me had been a lie' or 'And at that moment I lost my faith,' anything, in short, which might give a neat little artistic flourish to the end of this story. But there were other things I felt besides the initial surge of disgust and contempt for my father, which didn't last long in any case, since almost at once I started to feel sorry for him. What I want you to accept is this, that I knew *before* the driver turned round, that I saw it in that thin, auburn-haired woman's exhilaration as she began running down the path.

Ebba was still asleep when I got home. The last thing I wanted was for her to wake up and ask me what the matter was. I leaned over the bed and brushed a kiss on to her shoulder, vulnerably grateful to her for lying there. I felt myself shaking yet I was dry-eyed. Pity Dad thought I might, he wasn't to be wept over. Outside the window the sea glistened metallic against the soft curves of the dunes. Looking at it, I was reminded of my mother's desperate smile.

Les Osages or How We Cured the General of His Boredom

During the early months of 1826 all Europe – or at any rate that part of it with any pretensions to elegance, learning and the exact science of *comme il faut* – was thrown into convulsions by the news that Estifania Aboubacoula Tabaoula de Souffrière de la Cassonade had embarked, after several years of vexatious silence, upon another book. The first reports, disseminated in the form of rumours by different newspapers, declared that it was to be a novel, a successor perhaps to her vastly popular *La Sénégalaise* or its almost equally well-received sequel *La Fortune des Ouoloff*. Others hinted at the existence of a five-act tragedy, recalling those from which she had recited speeches before the astonished and admiring Empress at Malmaison, and founded upon certain events in the recent insurrection on the island of Santo Domingo. A few, more daring, suggested that Estifania might be on the point of publishing the amorous correspondence she had conducted with the young Milanese revolutionary Asdrubale Prosdocimo Opprandini, who had paid so miserably with his life during the failed uprising of 1821.

Whatever the truth of the matter, her celebrity was already so widely established that she hardly needed to publish anything more, and there were some who maintained, either through envy or malice, that she might have done better to stay silent, honourably embowered amid the garlands of critical esteem surrounding her earlier works. One grew, it must be said, a little weary of coming across her portrait, whether taken in profile by David d'Angers for his much-lauded bronze medal, or sketched by Lawrence as an engraved frontispiece for *The Keepsake*, or else in some copy of Fabre's thrilling likeness, where she appears *en déshabillé* against the background of a West Indian volcano (erupting), her chemise artistically unfastened to disclose the glistening loveliness of her shoulders and breasts, their blackness profound enough to be taken almost for a species of dark purple.

Black indeed Estifania was, and with this in mind I need hardly enter into more than the merest outline of an early life which, even before she started into print, was already a theme for the biographer. How she had been taken from the barracoons as a companion for his daughters by the benevolent planter Léonce de Souffriére de la Cassonade, friend of Lavoisier, translator of Lord Monboddo, author of an influential treatise on the use of succession-houses in the cultivation of shaddock, and despatched with them to France in the warship *Impitoyable*; how she had dazzled the Imperial kapellmeister Paisiello with her singing of an aria from his *I giochi de Agrifento* and mesmerised the assembled court at Malmaison with a Pindaric ode composed for the Emperor's birthday; how her Madras turbans had set a fashion *à la négresse* in the shops of the Palais-Royal, and how her assumption of her parents' African names had inspired the elderly *philosophe* Destutt de Tracy to write his *Système de la nomenclature* (alas no longer read); how, at the cessation of hostilities, she had visited England as the guest of an abolitionist riband manufacturer from Warrington, been fêted by the lady patronesses of Almack's and lionised at Holland House; how she had discussed pumice and fumaroles with Goethe at Weimar and baffled with her skill a celebrated *improvvisatrice* at Naples; how she posed for Canova's 'Niobe' and gave to Viganò the scenario for his ballet *Toussaint L'Ouverture* (suppressed at La Scala before its first performance) – all these things are too well known for me to need to dwell upon them here.

Of her lovers, what can be said? At fifteen she was courted by M. Martial Daru, son of the Emperor's secretary for war, whose libidinous ardour she wisely rejected in favour of the melancholy German Franz Xaver Ruffingfeld von Dornehl, later to shoot himself on the shore of the Lachersee after dedicating to her a volume of more than usually morbid speculation in verse on the likely outcome of their mutual passion. With a suitable discretion thereafter, Estifania launched herself into a sequence of affairs, each of which might have been thought to suggest itself as an inspiration for one or other of her literary productions, though none of them was unattended by the nagging possibility that the suitors concerned, the Milanese Carbonarist already mentioned, a Danish count, a Russian novelist and several of the *habitués* of Baron Cuvier's salon at the Jardin des Plantes, might only have been interested in her for the banal exoticism of her unquestionable colour and the corresponding bizarrerie, as they conceived it, of an African slave (notwithstanding M. de Souffrière's humane concession of her liberty on their arrival in Paris) engaged in the writing of novels and the construction of Voltairean dramas.

Irked by the supposition, and well provided for with funds left by her late master's wife, Estifania retreated to Italy, where she lived first of all at Florence and then, dismayed by the importunity of certain English and American ladies there who were desirous of securing her as the *clou* of their evening parties, retreated to Rome, settling in some handsomely furnished rooms in Via della Scrofa, in which she could be certain at any rate of some measure of obscurity, even as the only black female – for what she could tell – in the capital of the Papal States. For company she took with her merely the maid Victorine, loyal and trusted, who had entered her service at Mme de Souffrière's bidding many years previously. Eccentric as Estifania's solitariness must always have appeared to the Romans, it was never deemed outrageous, and since she was at home only to women, no sort of presumptuous masculine freedom assailed her almost hermit-like existence. Thus left alone, she began to write the book whose idea had absorbed her at intervals for more than a decade since one evening at Malmaison she had watched the duchesse d'Abrantès stifling a yawn.

It was to be a great History of Boredom, beginning with all its author might discover on the subject among the Greeks and Romans and extending, by way of the Middle Ages (in which, Estifania claimed, there was no such thing as a knowledge of dullness) and the seventeenth century (whose letters, memoirs and comedies offered rich proof of visitations by the demon Insipidity), to our own time, so amply furnished with occasions for tedium and so much given to expressing its peevishness at an existence hedged about with a profusion of numbing commonplaces. It was her belief – though she was prepared to find this challenged – that labour and religion had saved earlier societies from having to wrestle with boredom, but that the faculty of being bored had in itself been productive of some of the noblest artistic creations in those ages characterised by spiritual laxity and an excess of leisure. In this respect she evinced the reign of the Emperor Agustus, when, according to her theory, both Horace and Virgil had entered upon their poetic calling for the sake of beguiling an otherwise irksome idleness, and she had prepared a most spirited conclusion to the book in the figure of the late Lord Byron, driven to embrace Greek independence by the dreariness of a life already crowded with an excess of vicissitude.

Although Estifania's work was originally designed as an extensive chronicle of boredom and its causes during the passage of some two thousand years, she soon became determined to create a second volume which should study more closely the nature of the entire phenomenon as manifested among those around her. Such was her absorption in this new project that the grand historical survey was rapidly reduced to a single introductory chapter, and the *Histoire de l'ennui* was transformed into the accommodatingly vague *De l'ennui*, the title by which the book is nowadays known to its many admirers.

As the field of her latest researches, Rome at first seemed to offer the richest of materials. Slowly, and with admirable discretion, Estifania interviewed or secured the testimonies of several scores of persons as to their sensations and reactions in the face of all those things they professed to find even vestigially boring. The insufferable parade, affectation and languid verbal repetitiveness of an evening party, the torture of sitting next to a dinner companion without any conversation, and the comparable hideousness of spending three hours in the society of those who never drew breath, the frustrations of travel, the irksomeness of letter-writing, the numberless impositions on such nobler human faculties as patience, sympathy and compassion, and the vague but intriguing awareness some of her informants seemed to show regarding that sinister alliance between Boredom, Time and Ease, all these filled her notebooks until it must have seemed that she had more to work upon than might conveniently be digested even into two volumes. She examined intently all the bitter little anecdotes of weariness, monologues of disgust, sombre tales of dejection and aridity, catalogues of the soporific, the prosy, the flat and the humdrum, epics of defatigation, vignettes of satiety and lassitude, retailed to her either directly or else in the form of letters (always so surprisingly animated) by everybody from Neapolitan princes of the blood to the humblest nun within the meanest Roman convent.

Yet Estifania was not so far satisfied that she had discovered the true nature of boredom – enough of it, at any rate, to enable her to begin plotting its origins and progress in the form of a systematic treatise. The cause of her immediate dissatisfaction revealed itself one evening when, breaking with custom, she called for her carriage and went to the opera at the Teatro Argentina. Passionately devoted to music, she had long admired the talents of Mme Teresa Belloc, who was advertised that night as the prima donna in the lyric drama of *Redra* by Maestro Giovanni Simon Mayr, a composer for whose more serious works Estifania nursed a special predilection. Everything seemed designed at first to humour her expectancy on an occasion when the genius of the northern master and the brilliance of his interpreter (not eclipsed, as it had been at the opera's première some years before, by a popular rival) were combined to engage the capacity for feeling which Estifania, careful always to cultivate detachment in the course of her researches, had sedulously laid aside during the day.

If *Fedra* was to be the reward for her diligence, then poor Estifania suffered a cruel disappointment. To begin with, her appearance alone in her box created a most unwelcome degree of attention from the audience. Excited mutterings of very loud whispers of 'C'èl'Africana!' or 'E venuta la negra!' reminded her that, whatever their apparent pilotness, she was still an object of unquenchable curiosity to the Romans. She was accordingly visited in the box by an endless series of persons eager to claim her acquaintance, to press upon her yet more accounts of languor and morosity, or simply to be seen paying their respects to somebody hitherto noted for not going into society and for her steadfastness in refusing invitations from the most distinguished palaces in the city.

The pleasures of the opera were in consequence ruined. Even the beautiful 'Ah! fiero Ippolito', sung by the dying heroine to an exquisite accompaniment of soft violas and violoncellos with punctuations by the oboe, horn and bassoon, an air which Estifania herself had often played at her piano forte, was spoiled by the intrusion of an elderly *marchesa*, anxious to show off her attenuated son-in-law as the bored victim of over-indulgence in billiards and cigars. Such *corpora vilia* were not at that instant at all to Estifania's taste. The fair negress had laid aside her own science for one she must always consider more exalted, and was decidedly unwilling to be asked,at such a moment, to take it up again.

It was not these interruptions, however, which most unsettled Estifania so much as a general impression received from her scrutiny of the audience during the course of the evening. For were they not all of them bored to distraction? Looking about her at the vapid, simpering girls and the young men whose claims to originality and intelligence seemed to end at the point where each shirt collar, above a snowy, flawlessly tied cravat, met the edge of each smoothly barbered chin, at the film of cynicism and debauchery which covered the eyes of their fathers or their aunts, at the raised fan concealing the open mouth of a yawning chaperon, at the slouched form of somebody who had long ago resigned himself to snoring away ina *fauteuil* the sublimities of Mayr's opera, at heads threatening to totter into elbows, at jaws between which words emerged whose remoteness from meaning was of such a span that Estifania could almost catch them forming visibly in the air, at hands whose energetic gesticulation was inversely proportionate to the sincerity or validity of the sentiment they reinforced, she acknowledged with sudden horror the uselessness of making such a place as Italy the field in which her studies were to be most profitably carried forward. Boredom among the Italians, she perceived, so far from being singular occurence, its onslaughts infrequent enough to be remembered and examined, was something so necessary to existence as to be a perfectly vulgar instinct,whose promptings monopolized many of those energies which might otherwise have been devoted to the finer inducements of art,literature and politics.

She had barely left the theatre before the determination seized her to quit Italy for ever and journey northwards in quest of some place where boredom should matter for the thing it was, as opposed to being some gaseous component in the air which people breathed. For a few days afterwards she remained uncertain of where best to direct her steps, until one day, passing with Victorine through Via del Babuino and idly glancing into the window of a confectioner's shop, she saw, piled upon a stand at the very centre of the display, an assortement of crystallised plums. That afternoon she engaged a coachman, who told her of a travelling carriage newly put up for sale by a Russian admiral and his family, and the next morning she was the possessor of a magnificent *dormeuse* with fresh horses, here trunks were packed a portable writing desk had been placed inside the coach, and she was ready to set off for the very place in which those plums had first achieved their sugary preservation.

Estifania felt no special pangs at leaving a land where she had expended so much in the way of emotion and curiosity to, as she now felt, so little purpose. As short a time as possible, therefore, was passed in saying adieu to the various places along the route which were marked by her personal experiences of happiness, profound contemplation or occasional misery. Her coachman Pasquale had manifested at once a capacity for slavish devotion to her well-being and seemed to understand, if not the reasons for her leaving Italy, then at least the urgency they demanded, and it was not long before the fir-clad slopes of the Tirol closed about them and Estifania, with a little shudder of excitement, heard the first German spoken in the villages.

She slipped into Carlsbad at three in the morning, and put up at the Goldener Schild und Zwei Deutsche Monarchen on the Neue Wiese. It was the end of April, the Season had not yet opened, and for several ensuing weeks she was able to resume, amid the pine-clad hills along the Tephl, the quiet tenor of existence she had enjoyed in Rome, though with a more assured tranquillity and freedom from interruption. Each morning she spent in the reading room at the Kurhaus before walking to one of the springs, the Sprudel, the Mühlbrunnen or the Stefanie-Queelle for preference, to drink a glass or two of water and listen to the band for luncheon. Following her hours of rest during the afternoon she strolled to the Cafe Sanssouci, or to the Posthof with its pleasant garden, where over tea and a plate of *oplatky* wafers or a slice of *Brunnenkuchen*, she was able to observe those portions of *le monde ou l'on s'amuse* slowly gathering to perform their annual rites of penance for the ten or eleven previous months spent in over-indulgence and debauchery.

On these occasions Estifania's blackness proved more of an advantage than a hindrance whenever she needed to secure further material for her examination of the ever-engrossing theme. Struck by her restrained yet always unstudied elegance and that expression, beautifully caught in Lawrence's engraving, of sympathetic attentiveness to those who addressed her, persons of all kinds, after the briefest of conversations, declared themselves ready to answer the little printed questionnaire she set in front of them, its simple list of interrogatives meant to form the basis for a kind of brief, intimate history of the subject's acquaintance with dullness.

As the season gathered momentum during early June, the stream of miniature autobiographies occasioned by Estifania's questioning swelled into a perfect flood. She had been correct, she soon realised, in her calculation that a spa of all places must be the ideal repository for every sort of recollected experience connected with those different aspects of tedium and frustration she was so bent on pulling to pieces. The hours of enforced and regulated idleness, the care taken to ensure that amusement of whatever kind should not be judged synonymous in the smallest degree with dissipation, and the organised innocence of a society in which everybody was tucked up in bed by eleven o'clock at night, were each of them an encouragement to concentration and detailed exactitude among those who proffered their various kinds of testimony. By the end of the month she had amassed more than enough material to begin work on the the oretical portion of the *magnum opus*, and was correspondingly grateful to Carlsbad for the liberality with which it was thus obliged her. The place seemed a veritable Patmos, in which she sat poised to make her book of revelation.

One feature alone threatened to muddle the perfection of her design. She had yet to meet, amid the fashionable throng which fretted its hour along the Wiese, a single person who should sincerely confess to never having been bored, if not in the whole course of existence, then at least for a great many years. Though part of her was sceptical as to the possibility of finding any such figure, she endeavoured to convince herself that people of this kind existed, and the supposition began slightly to unsettle an otherwise agreeable composure. She started discreetly to ask about among the multitude of acquaintance formed in the course of her enquiries, but no one, it seemed, knew of anybody who had not at some time or another been even mildly bored.

It was when, late one afternoon, Estifania was walking from her hotel to take her daily glass or two at the springs that she hit upon a possible answer. The pavement was not especially crowded, and hence she was more inclined to notice those who passed or were walking ahead of her – a shabby-looking female carrying a basket of cherries, a tall girl in a blue dress with a book in her hand, and two hotel servants carrying a placard announcing the iminent arrival of a pair of acrobats. Struck by a detail in the trimming adorning the bonnet of a woman in front of her, Estifania drew a little closer, and, able thus to overhear snatches of the conversation between this person and her companion, she found herself reluctant to forgo the opportunity.

'My husband declares he has never met anybody more exasperating in his entire life.'

'Simply because the wretched man will never complain about anything? Come now!'

'True, I assure you. Someone the other day at Lady Jersey's asked him what he was interested in, and would you believe that he answered in all sincerity: "Madame, everything"? How can one entertain such a monster?'

'You forget, *ma chère*, that he has travelled and seen much, and that sort of man can never be bored.'

'Pooh, nonsense, there are plenty of men in Carlsbad who have experienced twice or three times what he has seen or known, and most of them are bored to death for the best part of the day.'

Unable to restrain herself any further, and feeling in any case that she must cut a curious figure as she dogged the two women along the pavement, Estifania made herself known to them and explained her predicament in relation to what she had just heard. The situation they found amusing, so much so that they were prepared to rack their memories for every possible morsel of evidence as to this paragon, so blissfully untouched by ennui yet, it appeared, so mysteriously exasperating for that very reason to those about him. This latter aspect Estifania found hardest of all to credit. She was more interested by the exact means through which he had secured his singular invulnerability, and, thanking the two ladies for their kindness, she returned to her hotel determined to write requesting an interview.

Her letter was answered with the most flattering promptness. The paragon would be happy to wait upon her tomorrow afternoon at three o'clock at her hotel, and to furnish her with whatever information she might require. He had heard, he acknowledged, of her researches into the nature of boredom, and would consider it an honour to be of use, at however humble a level, in a scheme of enquiry so obviously conducive to the advancement of scientific understanding. He could readily appreciate the surprise she must feel at his claim, stoutly maintained, never to have been bored for upwards of thirty years. He was used to encountering scepticism on this subject, but a few details would be sufficient to set everything right. Delighted once again to be of service, he had the pleasure of signing himself, etc.etc. Estifania could scarcely credit her good fortune.

When he arrived on the following day, punctual to his

hour, General Count Langweil von Oehde of the Twenty-third Imperial Chasseurs at any rate looked the part – and Estifania, who, we should remember, had been introduced to the great world at the court of Napoleon Bonaparte, knew what a general was supposed to look like. At sixty-five he appeared remarkably trim and well-preserved, and Estifania acknowledged herself quite taken by his distinctive air of absolute candour mixed with straight forward common sense. They talked or rather he talked to her, for some time about the West Indies, which of course he had visited, the superiority of Guinea negroes as a racial type to those of Angola, their general laziness as a breed and their fondness for dancing and heathen religions. The General had heard the *gnädige Fräulein* mentioned as a novelist. He didn't care much for modern novels, but he had written a couple himself and was sure there was nothing she could tell him about the difficulties entailed of keeping the plot bowling nicely along. Women, she must agree, had been much overrated as novelists. There had been an English woman, of one of whose works the Empress Marie Louise – ah yes, he knew her Imperial Majesty, now Duchess of Parma – had been so kind as to lend him a translation, something about a girl in a village trying to find husbands for all the other women and a lot of nonsense about picnics and strawberry-picking, but he'd thought the whole thing deucedly insipid, a man could never have written such stuff. Most people were in awe of writers, but the General had never been afraid of them. Had the *gnädige Fräulein* ever met in Goethe? Oh, she had, had she? Well, the General certainly had, here at Carlsbad, and let him tell her, the Herr Geheimrat von Goethe wasn't a bit frightening, only a shade pompous, that was all, and the General had been most happy to set him right over a question of modern artillery drill.

But the *gnädige Fräulein* must be getting bored with ... Bored, ah yes! the General had almost forgotten what he was going to tell her, their conversation had been so interesting.

Was she ready to hear it? Estifania signified her inclination with a polite nod. And the General began as follows:

'It must have been – let me see – around the year 1782 when my uncle, the Court Chamberlain to our Emperor Joseph, requested His Majesty to send me, for the purpose of completing my education, to Paris as part of the entourage of the Austrian Ambassador. I was twenty-one, not yet pledged to my military vocation, and to all intents and purposes extremely susceptible to the charms of a city which in those days might have been considered the capital of Europe. The duties of a young attaché were more nominal than actual, I had a splendid suite of rooms in a house near the convent of the Minimes and a handsome monthly allowance from my family, paid to me by the Ambassador in person. The entrée to all the great salons of the city was mine, I was routinely invited to concerts, operas, card parties, balls, *petits soupers* and *fêtes champêtres*, and every tradesman in the town solicited my credit for the most extravagant of commodities. I ought to have been happy, yet I was not.

The cause of my misery was the descent upon me, in early youth, of an abysmally profound inability to be interested in anything whatsoever. I was of course highly intelligent and physically agile, so that I easily excelled in those pursuits in which boys of my age are required to shine. I was a fine shot, I sat a horse very well, I ran and climbed trees and in due time showed myself a first-rate dancer. I acquired Latin and Greek without difficulty, mastered the principles of mathematics and conversed fluently in several of the European languages. My father's favourite diversion was the violoncello, which he played in string quartets with Vanhal and Ditters von Dittersdorff, and for a time I took up the violin with the object of joining him, but though my masters showered compliments upon my taste and aptness, even music proved at last an insufficient distraction.

Paris, as I have said, offered no prospect of relieving the miasmal tedium. In France one is expected to engage in sentimental affairs, and the Ambassador encouraged me to take a mistress – several indeed, for the amusement of playing them off against one another. Nature has made me good-looking, and this, added to the elegance and manliness of my address, at once recommended me to some of the handsomest women then admired at the court of Versailles, several of them in attendance on the unfortunate Queen, who, you may recall, was herself an Austrian princess and thus not disposed to look unkindly upon me.

Love, however, was no more a palliative than music or exercise might have been before I left Austria. Each morning I rose to greet the daylight in a condition approaching numbness, a sort of moral desiccation which made any species of sympathetic reaction to the plight of others almost impossible. Unexcited, hardly more alert to what surrounded me than a corpse might have been if lifted from the coffin, dead, as it were, before I had travelled a bare portion of my journey to the grave, I moved incuriously through the waking hours, treating everything as a sequence of formal gestures and motions and speaking to people, I am told, in a voice strangely devoid of tone or inflection, that of a ghost in a play – yet even stage ghosts discourse with a greater animation than I apparently was then capable of.

My friends – for of course I had a great many friends – were seriously alarmed by my condition, which I did not scruple to discuss with them. I became the object not merely of their solicitude but of the scientific inquisitiveness of certain doctors they called in to examine me and who proposed a whole variety of treatments, from the application of magnets to different parts of my body to a device whereby I remained suspended by my feet from the ceiling, under careful supervision, for brief periods during the day in order to stimulate the flow of blood to the brain.

None of these well-intentioned schemes had the desired effect. I was as bored as before. The summer arrived, and with it several – I should say a great many – invitations to visit the châteaux of my Parisian acquaintance. Without enthusiasm I found myself in Normandy, at a house not far from the sea coast on the eastern side of the peninsula of Cotentin. My hosts, M. and Mme de D——were aware of my condition, but there was this difference in their behaviour towards me, as opposed to that of others, that they did not undertake any sort of cure, let alone propose any amusement with the deliberate idea of rousing me from lassitude or insipidity. I was allowed to do more or less as I pleased, wandering about the grounds of the château, spending hours in the library, riding down to the sea, and only required for civility's sake to join the family at meals. My reluctance to accompany them when, for example, they went off to a nearby town to visit a travelling menageries or wild beast show reported as having arrived there, or when, out of curiosity, they intended driving to a neighbouring castle where, it was said, a deputation of mandarins from the Emperor of China had halted on its way to Paris, was quite understood, and for several days I felt something almost like happiness occasioned by the tactful restraint with which my friends chose to treat me.

One morning, nevertheless, the D——s contrived, as it were, to outwit me – for the question, of course, is always whether boredom is intentional or purely instinctive, and I as sometimes of the opinion that mine was of the former variety. Mme de D——, at luncheon, giving a loud yawn, proclaimed that she was most dreadfully fagged and hipped and in need of a drive. Her husband declared himself ready to accompany her, but was strict in his proviso that on this occasion they should not have to call upon anybody or do anything that should entail having to converse with anyone except each other. Struck by this sudden particularity and very mildly surprised at either of them appearing familiar for even a moment with a state of being which seemed mine for eternity, I asked whether, if this really were the project, I might come with them, on the assumption that none of us should speak a word more than was necessary. They both agreed readily to the idea, and in silence we set off through the countryside.

Our shared taciturnity endured without interruption for almost an hour. The coachman seemed to have gauged our mood, and followed those roads least frequented by other vehicles, or ones which skirted villages where we might have been exposed to the obsequious salutations of the country people as we passed. Again a faint impression of pleasure began settling upon me, simply because my friends appeared so perfectly to have understood my present disposition and in some measure to have contracted it themselves. It was wonderful to me to know that there might be others who experienced what I did and with whom at last I should be able rationally to discuss my intense absence of sensation.

Such complacency could not survive long. With remarkable dexterity the driver had managed to bring the coach down to the very edge of the seashore before I was even aware of it, and to my horror I found that we now sat overlooking a small crowd of people from every class of society, watching in amazement the sight which presented itself upon the beach, under a bright but not oppressive sun, in a sky across which a bracing breeze drove the little plump whorls of cloud.

At the centre of the prospect laythe gigantic greyish-black form of a sperm whale, *Physeter macrocephalus*, which, having somehow managed to beach itself at the high tide, was now either dead or dying, its immense squared-off nose still seeming to twitch somewhat as flocks of seabirds screamed and swooped around it, with the myriad scars and indentations so characteristic of the breed clearly visible across its glistening sides.

Surrounding this extraordinary object was what I might term a picturesque grouping formed of humans and animals. To the right, that is to say closest to the large posterior flukes of the creature, stood an elephant, attended by two mahouts, on whose back rode a collection of half-naked figures in feathered bonnets whom a second glance enabled me to identify as Red Indians (as I later learned, from the Osage tribe). On the other side, sagely contemplating the whale's mouth and eyes, was a throng of Chinamen, dressed in the most exquisite long-sleeved silken robes, with embroidered slippers, conical hats and the pigtails appropriate to their rank. Behind them, at a respectful distance, stood a dignified-looking Egyptianwith moustachios of luxuriant growth, holding by the halter a giraffe of singular grace and subtlety of colour.

In an instant I had leapt from the carriage and pushed towards the edge of the crowd. My friends had of course known exactly where it was they were taking me, and their good sense had judged the effect precisely. In an instant, at the merest glimpse of such a prodigy as the vision of these things thus flung together on the shore then seemed to me, my boredom vanished into air, and since then it has ever, in the slightest sense, returned. The scene, complete with the whale, the Osages, the mandarins, the elephant and the giraffe, was re-created a few years ago by one of our most skilful artists and now occupies a place of honour at my residence on the Oehdeberg. So that, *Gnädige Fräulein*, is, you see ...'

But Estifania wasnot listening. She had been asleep for some time. It was thus, an hour or so later, that the faithful Victorine found her mistress in repose upon the sofa, with one of the hotel's cats settled comfortably under the crook of her arm. The General, much too interested to notice, had long since slipped away.